HOLD HIM CLOSE

J.P. BOWIE

Hold Him Close
ISBN # 978-1-83943-986-5

Interior text design by Claire Siemaszkiewicz
Pride Publishing

Published in 2021 by Pride Publishing, United Kingdom.

Pride Publishing is an imprint of Totally Entwined Group Limited.

Pride Publishing books by J.P. Bowie

Single Books

The Set Up
Ride 'em Cowboy
Ride 'em Again Cowboy
Personal Trainers
Halloween Angel
The Officer and the Gentleman
With a Little Help from My Friends
Blood Relations
Nowhere to Hide
Trip of a Lifetime
A Ghost Story
Happy Ending
A Highlander in LA
Journey to Hope
Paris Connection
All I'll Ever Need
Every Breath I Take
Highland Hearts
Evan Sent
Fear and Loving in Las Vegas
Breaking the Habit
Fear of Flying
Love on the Rocks
Murder by Design
The Love Between Us
Hold Him Close

My Vampire and I

My Vampire and I
My Vampire Lover
Duet in Blood
Blood Resurrection
Bound in Blood
Blood Lure
Blood Lust
Blood Talisman

Blood Vigilance
Blood Kiss

The Journeyer
The Journey Begins
The New World
The Fight for Freedom
Into the West

Hot in the Saddle
Vetting the Cowboy
Teaching the Cowboy
Loving the Cowboy
Naming the Cowboy

Anthologies
Fabulous Brits: Under the Law
Naughty Nooners: Lunches in Laguna
Friction: Cruising
Saddle Up 'N' Ride: Ride 'em Hard Cowboy
Promoted by the Billionaire: Fly to Him
Heatwave: Summer Bliss

Collections
Christmas Spirits: A Present Christmas
Homecoming: Blueprint for Love
Yule Be Mine: A Special Christmas
Immortal Love: Night Wing
A Little Bit Cupid: Valentine's Day Blues
My Bloody Valentine: Dark Valentine

HOLD HIM CLOSE

Dedication

My thanks and appreciation to Claire Siemaszkiewicz, Rebecca Scott and everyone at Pride Publishing for their continued support, and to my esteemed editor, Rebecca Baker, for her ability to make my stories just that much better—and error free!

To my husband, Phil, my endless devotion.

Chapter One

John White Eagle parked his Harley outside the building where he rented his office space and sprinted up the stairs, glancing at his phone as he took the steps two at a time.

"Good morning, John." Millie Barnum, his secretary, greeted him with a bright smile.

"Morning, Millie. Anything urgent?"

"Just the message I'm guessing you're reading on your phone right now."

"Huh. You're right. But I just left Mark at home. What can he want already?"

"That's not for me to speculate on." Millie, gray-haired, bespectacled, her appearance more suited to a school principal's office than his slightly less-than-upscale space, stared at him with sparkling blue eyes. "What you boys get up to is certainly none of my business, thank goodness."

"Riiight. You'd love it if I gave you the deets on what goes on at Chez Rossi/White Eagle. But that's not going to happen. Mark and I are not taking the place of the characters you read about on your Kindle. At least not with an audience."

"I like your hair grip," Millie said, ignoring his comment about her love of male romantic fiction.

"I found it in a box when Mark and I moved into the new house in North Hollywood. My grandmother made it for me and I'd forgotten I even had it still." He slipped a hand to the back of his head and fingered the intricate pattern of small beads. "It's neat, isn't it?"

Millie got up to take a closer look. "It's beautiful. She must have had such a delicate touch." She sighed. "And you have hair that's far too lovely to be on a man. Anyway, you'd better get in touch with Mark right now. He sounded irritated that you hadn't returned his call."

"How the hell can he be irritated within the space of a half-hour since I left him?"

Millie pursed her lips. "Did you perhaps forget to kiss him goodbye?"

John chuckled. "As if. We might've been together for ten years, but he never lets me outta the house without savaging my mouth first."

"Oh, my." Millie clutched at her bosom. "The vision *that* just conjured up. Savaging, oh my." She did a pretend stagger back to her desk, making John laugh. *How did I ever get so lucky as to find a woman like Millie?* Totally efficient on the computer and phone, but also unfazed by the high and the very low life that sometimes waltzed through the doors of JWE Investigations, looking for some kind of help, legal or otherwise. Then there was the fact that John just happened to be a gay man.

He'd explained that to her when she'd answered his ad and met him for an interview. *"Just so you know, I'm gay and Native American,"* he'd told her. *"If you have a problem with either one, say so now."*

"I'll have you know I am neither a racist nor a bigot," she'd replied. *"In fact, when I was a young girl, I used to cheer for the Indians in those old westerns…still do, when they repeat them on late-night TV."*

She'd been less impressed with his office and had suggested that he give it a good coat of paint. *"I have some nice prints I can bring in, and a couple of plants by the window will certainly give the place a little more ambience, don't you think?"*

"I think I've been taken over by a formidable force," he'd told Mark when he'd gotten home that night. Mark had laughed but had helped him paint the office and given his full approval of Millie's efficiency, and the set of Norman Rockwell prints she'd brought with her to brighten the walls.

She'd fallen in love with Mark at first sight. Not that John could be surprised by that. His husband was an amiable man, and movie-star gorgeous. They'd met when John had been set up to take the fall in a murder perpetrated by Greg Mathis, a then-famous actor who'd told John he was being blackmailed. Mathis had convinced John to go with him to a motel room to confront the blackmailer. Except, unbeknownst to John, the blackmailer was already dead, in the bathroom tub.

Mathis had told John the blackmailer hadn't shown, but he'd coerced John into bed after handing him a drugged beer. Unaware of the beer being drugged, John hadn't needed much coaxing into the offer of sex with Mathis. He'd been young, horny and still starry-eyed about his involvement with such a big celebrity, even admiring the man's acting ability. In addition, Greg Mathis had been one of the most gorgeous men on the planet. As a matter of fact, he'd been nominated The Planet's Sexiest Man more than once in a popular magazine. Alone with him in the room, John had wondered at Mathis' eagerness to be fucked by him, insisting on going through with it even though John had been aware he wasn't enjoying it at all. That look of pain had never morphed into one of pleasure.

When John had regained consciousness, the police had been hammering at the motel room's door. The arresting officer, Detective Mark Rossi, had appeared to believe John's story under interrogation, even if he wouldn't divulge the name of the man he'd been with. John had been convinced no one would believe that Greg Mathis, super-macho movie star, could possibly be involved in such sleaze, but he'd reckoned without Mark totally seeing the truth in John's story.

John had never dreamed that being arrested by Mark would later result in a dinner date with the handsome cop, and the mind-blowing sex that had followed. Those first bleak days when it had looked as if John were the only suspect, and the evidence against him had grown stronger, had only been tempered by Mark's insistence that he'd believed John's story.

Sometimes he wondered why his mind dwelled on that incident so often. He supposed it was because it had been the defining moment in his life. Mark had been with him throughout the ordeal, even when things had taken a decided downturn the day forensics had called Mark with the news that the sperm in the condom they'd found in the dead man's rectum was a match for John's DNA. It had been a measure of Mark's faith in John's innocence that he'd believed in him, despite that damning evidence.

His cell chimed with Mark's ringtone. *Oops, now he'll be more than just irritated.*

"John!" Millie's voice from the main office held an accusatory tone. She knew Mark's ringtone too. "Haven't you called Mark yet?"

"Picking up now! Hi, sweetie, what's up?"

"Don't 'hi, sweetie' me." Mark sounded pissed, and not improved by John's quiet chuckle. "Hey, I've called a dozen times at least."

"No you haven't. Three times by my reckoning."

"Then why the hell haven't you responded? Don't you know what day it is?"

"Uh, it's Thursday, isn't it?"

"It's my dad's birthday, smartass."

"Fuck. Why didn't you say something before I left the house?"

"Because...because I forgot about it, too—till about twenty minutes ago."

"Oh good. That makes me feel better."

"*John...*"

He could almost feel the heat of Mark's glare through the phone. *Oh, that hot Italian blood.* His cock pulsed in his briefs at the thought of Mark's lush lips on his. "Sorry, didn't mean to be flippant. Call him and say we're taking him out to dinner—and how on earth could he have forgotten? I'll pick up a card and a bottle of his favorite Scotch."

"Okay, you are redeemed in my eyes. What about the restaurant?"

"I'll leave that to you. He doesn't like fancy, remember."

"Louie's Pub?"

"Perfect. Okay, man I love above all others on earth, I have to make like I'm working. Let me know the time I need to meet you."

Mark chuckled. "You sure know how to blow some hot air up my ass."

"That's not all I know about what to do with your ass," John said slyly. "Your mighty fine ass…an ass that belongs on the body of a much younger man, I might add."

"Thank you, I think."

"You can compliment *my* ass later. Gotta go. Ciao."

"Ciao, baby. Love you."

"Love you too." From the start of their relationship, John had insisted they end their phone conversations with that sentiment. Not that he wanted to be morbid, but Mark's career did involve an element of danger and it would kill John if something happened to Mark and he hadn't heard those words that day. *I'm a sentimental sap, I know, but there it is…*

Millie sighed happily in the outer office.

"You shouldn't eavesdrop, you know, Millie. It might sully your innocence."

She barked out a sardonic laugh but didn't say anything. John heard the door open and Millie say sweetly, "How can I help you?"

"Is Mr. Eagle in?" The voice was female and tentative.

"Do have an appointment with Mr. White Eagle, my dear?"

"No, but if he's busy I can come back…"

"Just one moment."

Millie stuck her head around John's door. "You want to take this?" she whispered. "She looks sad."

John groaned mentally. Most likely another suspicious wife wanting to find out who her errant husband was screwing when he was not at home with her and the kids. Some said that kind of investigating was the bread and butter of the business, but John hated it. There were so many disappointed and unhappy couples out there. It often made him feel guilty that he and Mark were so happy…most of the time. One thing was for sure—if the impossible ever happened, and Mark cheated on him, he wouldn't have to hire a private detective to find out.

Swallowing his inappropriate laughter, he said, "Okay, I'll come out." He got up from his desk and followed Millie as she approached the young woman standing nervously by the door. She was very young—early twenties, John guessed—and pale. Pale skin, pale blonde hair, eyebrows and eyelashes. Very little makeup. She wore a rose-pink blouse and a gray skirt, and clutched at a large bag slung over her left shoulder. A quick glance told John she wasn't wearing a wedding ring. *So maybe not the problem I first thought she had.*

"Hi." He held out his hand. "I'm John White Eagle."

After a moment's hesitation, she put her small hand in his. "P-Penny Andrews. I don't have an appointment, but I wondered if I could speak with you for a few minutes?"

"Of course. Come on through. Would you like some coffee? Millie makes a wonderful cup."

"Just some water, please. It's a little warm outside today."

"I'll get that for you," Millie said, walking over to the cooler.

John shepherded Miss Andrews into his office and indicated the seat opposite his. He waited until Millie had set a glass of water in front of her then left before he asked, "So how can I help you?"

"My brother is missing, and I think someone may have killed him."

John stared at her for a moment. Thar was not what he'd expected her to say at all. "What makes you think that?"

"I haven't seen him or been able to contact him in over a week." She took a Kleenex out of her bag and passed it over her face briefly.

John had noticed the fine beads of sweat on her forehead and upper lip. *Maybe she isn't feeling well.* "And that's unusual?"

She nodded. "Yes. We are really, really close. We have been all our lives. Even when he was married, hardly a day went by that we didn't talk at some point. We also meet up at least once a week for lunch. He works for Brennan Finance, downtown. I only work part-time, at a bookstore, so I take the bus to meet him."

"And did you have a lunch date he didn't show for?"

She nodded. "I wasn't able to reach him for two days, but I went to our favorite diner near his office building on our regular day, and he didn't show up. I called and called and went round to his apartment in Silver Lake. He didn't answer my knocking. I asked his neighbor who he does some chores for if she'd seen him, and she said not since Friday, when he took her trash out. That was a week ago today."

"Have you contacted the police to report him missing?"

"Oh, no. They'd most likely want to contact my father and I'm afraid that if they questioned him, he'd go ballistic."

John frowned. "Why would he go ballistic? Would he not be worried like you are about his disappearance?"

She hesitated then said, "Sam and our father don't get along. In fact, they hate each other. I'm afraid they might have gotten into some kind of fight. That happens a lot. They both have a temper, but our father can be violent. Not so much since Sam has grown up and can defend himself, but it used to be bad, and now..."

"Are you afraid of your father, Miss Andrews?"

She looked away and passed the tissue over her eyes, then nodded. "Sometimes. I don't think he'd ever hurt me physically, but he yells when he's mad...and he says some terrible things."

"Like?"

"Like I killed my mother. She died as a result of giving birth to me, he says. I was three when she died, but he said she was never the same after I was born, that she'd gone through hell in labor and he'd known she'd never really recover from the trauma."

Jeez... John already hated Mr. Andrews. *What kind of a creep throws that in his daughter's face?* Especially as the girl had lost her mother at such an early age. And from the sound of it, he'd been doing it for a long time. He could see the toll it had taken on the young woman. She was so frail and nervous. Verbal abuse could be as hurtful as the physical kind. Detective Mark Rossi could attest to that from the countless abuse cases he'd dealt with.

"The truth is, Mr. White Eagle..." Her posture and voice seemed to shrink as she continued. "Although I pray he did not, I think my father might've killed Sam. Perhaps not deliberately, but by accident during one of their rows. Like I said, he has a terrible temper. He might have struck out at Sam. Perhaps not really meaning to kill him, but somehow…it happened."

"That's some accusation, Miss Andrews." John frowned. "Could it not be that your brother simply wanted to get away for some personal reasons? Girlfriend trouble, maybe? Didn't want anyone to know until he was ready to talk about it? There could be a hundred reasons why."

She shook her head. "He wouldn't want me to worry about him. He would tell me if was just going away for a time."

"You seem so sure about that." John drummed his fingers on the top of his desk. "Do you know everything about your brother's state of mind, or his personal life?"

"I know enough," she replied sharply. "Enough to know he has no girlfriend."

"Boyfriend, then?"

She shook her head again. "He's not gay. He was married at one time, for a year."

John wasn't about to give her a lecture on the 'low-down' so many married men indulged in when they wanted a brief time out from their marriage. Instead he asked, "You're sure? I thought that might be the reason you want to employ a gay private detective."

"No. I came to you because of an article about you in *Vanity Fair*, where you were instrumental in finding a young girl who'd been missing for several weeks. You succeeded where the police could not."

"That's not exactly true," John said. "I had a lot of help from a detective sergeant in the LAPD. It was a joint effort."

She nodded. "A detective sergeant who worked off the clock to help you…your husband."

"That's correct. *VF* tended to downplay Mark's involvement—at his request, I might add. Nevertheless, it was a joint success, and might have ended differently had he not been at my side."

"The article was better than some of the books I've read." Miss Andrews was almost gushing. She gazed at John through watery eyes. "Will you please take my case? Find out what has happened to Sam?"

"I will," John assured her. "But what makes you think your father might have actually killed your brother…his son? What could your bro have possibly done to bring that kind of reaction from your dad?"

"I really don't know. Sam didn't say anything about having a recent argument with him, or that they were more at odds than usual. Sam works for our father at his company. Father bought out the owners of Brennan Finance a couple of years ago. It might have had something to do with work. Sam tends to regard Brennan as being a bit cutthroat toward some of the less affluent clients, and also as secondary to what he really loves doing, but he would've told me if there'd have been a problem there."

"What is it he really loves doing?" John asked.

She smiled. "He's a bit of an adventurer. Loves going to foreign lands, researching cultures, that kind of thing."

"So, couldn't that be what he's doing right now?"

"Yes, but as I said, he wouldn't just go off without letting me know, especially if it was out of the country."

She seemed pretty certain about this, so John thought it best to switch the line of questioning. "Have you asked your father if he knows where Sam is?"

"Yes, and he sort of fluffed it off. He said he didn't have a clue. Then he added that he didn't really care either. It was as if it didn't matter to him."

"Nice guy..."

She dabbed at her eyes again. "No, he's not a nice guy, Mr. White Eagle. He's my father, but I'm afraid there isn't much of a loving father-daughter relationship between us. I couldn't pretend otherwise."

Clutching at the large bag she held on her lap, she bit her lip. "Oh, I'm sorry. You certainly don't need to hear about any of that. Please find my brother, or find out what happened to him. I can pay your fee, whatever it is. It's killing me not knowing where he is."

"All right." John was okay taking the case, but she had to know he couldn't proceed without confronting Andrews Senior. "However, I have to warn you that the first person I'm going to talk to is your father. In my opinion, he has got to know something about your brother's whereabouts. They work together, or rather your brother works for him. Would he not have run by your father the fact he needed time off?"

She frowned. "He won't like you asking questions."

John smiled. "I'm kinda used to that aspect of the job. Let me have your brother's cell number, and do you have a photo of him, by any chance?"

"Uh, yes, but it's the only one I have in my bag. I hate to give it up."

"That's okay. Millie will make a copy for me."

"Oh, okay." She rifled through the contents of her bag then produced a business card from her wallet and handed it to John. "His cell and office numbers are on the card...and here's his photo."

Whoa... John involuntarily widened his eyes as he gazed at the photo Penny had given him. The guy was a looker, without a doubt. Blond, like his sister, but with stronger features, clear blue eyes and full lips that were parted in a killer smile that showed off straight, white teeth.

"He's handsome, isn't he?"

John flicked his gaze back to Penny Andrews. "Yes, he is. Okay, I'll take on your case and I'll do my best to give you peace of mind about your brother. I'll need a check up front for two days of my time, but Millie will take care of all that for you. If I find out where your bro is within a day, I'll refund half the check amount. If it takes more than two days then it's on a daily basis, but I'll keep you apprised of my progress each day."

"That sounds fair." She followed him to Millie's desk to write the check and waited for Millie to photocopy her brother's picture. "Thank you for taking this on. And please, find Sam for me…safe and sound if possible."

John smiled and held out his hand, taking hers gently. "I'll do my best, Miss Andrews." He showed her out then returned to his desk. He fingered Sam's business card for a beat or two then picked up his phone and called the man's cell number. *No harm in trying…* After a couple of rings, he was directed to Sam's voicemail.

"Oh, hi. My name is John White Eagle. I'm a private detective, and your sister, Penny, hired me to find you. She is concerned for your safety. Please, either call her or return my call so that I can verify your whereabouts with her. Would appreciate a prompt reply. Thank you."

Okay, so his phone is still active…let's see if he still is.

"So, what do you think, Millie?" he asked, after he'd given her a quick rundown of the conversation with Penny Andrews.

His secretary sighed. "From what you've told me, I think she's a very unhappy girl, something I saw in her before she even spoke to you. If it turns out that her brother has been killed, it will be devastating for her. But don't you think she's far too dependent on him? This over-insistence on how close they are seems strange to me. Could she be holding something back?"

John nodded. "Yeah, I got that too. Interesting case. I think my first course of action will be to pay a surprise visit to the creepy father."

"Better you than me," Millie said snippily. "I can already tell that he and I would not have a friendly conversation."

John grinned. "Know what you mean, but I'll try not to be too in his face."

Chapter Two

Brennan Finance was on Century Boulevard. It shared the building with a variety of finance and escrow businesses. The lobby teemed with businesspeople of all genders, all smartly dressed and looking resolute. The elevator that sped John up to the seventeenth floor was packed with silent men and women all busy staring at their phones or punching in text messages.

The young girl at reception gazed at John with wide eyes when he approached her desk.

"It's the hair and the cheekbones," Mark had told him early on in their relationship, when John had asked why he thought people stared at him so often.

"Are they intimidated by me, d'you think?" he'd asked.

"Only by your beauty. Makes them feel inferior."

"Okay, Mr. Silver Tongue. You know where that kind of talk leads..."

John freed himself from his inappropriate thoughts of Mark and sex, and smiled back at the receptionist. She had buckteeth that seemed to make her smile all the more appealing. "Hi, I'm John White Eagle and I'd like to see Mr. Andrews."

"Your name is really John White Eagle? Like you're an Indian?"

John fixed his gaze on her name tag, which read *Mandy*. "Native American, Mandy…yes, I am. Dakota Sioux. Is Mr. Andrews available?"

"Oh, sorry, let me just check for you." She picked up her phone and punched in a two-digit number. "Cindi, there's a gentleman here to see Mr. Andrews." She listened for a moment than asked John, "May we ask the reason for your visit?"

"I'd like some advice."

"He'd like some financial advice."

John suppressed a grin.

"Uh, yes, it's a Mr. White Eagle." She looked up at John. "I'll take you over to Mr. Andrews' office."

Mandy opened a door into a large space crowded with cubicles. John shuddered. No way could he work in a place like this. His office might be tight, but at least there were only him and Millie sharing it. He was conscious of lots of stares as he followed Mandy past the many desks. Mostly women, but he caught a couple of guys also giving him loaded looks. Mandy tapped on the frosted glass of a door marked *Evan Andrews CEO* then pushed it open.

"Hi, Cindi. This is Mr. White Eagle to see Mr. Andrews."

A tall brunette stood and walked toward John, holding out a hand in greeting. Her black dress was stylish, but John wondered how on earth she could walk without teetering in those impossibly high heels. She seemed to manage just fine, though.

"Mr. White Eagle," she said, grasping his hand. "I've never met anyone with such an exotic name before. Is it a pen name? Are you a writer?"

Her intense gaze took in every inch of John's frame, from his face to his boots and most definitely everything in between. It wasn't often that John was made to feel uncomfortable by someone obviously staring too long, but this woman came close. He took her hand for the briefest of shakes and dropped it as her fingers curled over his palm.

"I'm not a writer," John told her, "and it is my real name…the family name for hundreds of years. Is Mr. Andrews available?"

She frowned. "No, Mr. Andrews is not available today. Can one of our other consultants help you?"

"How about Sam Andrews…is he available?" John asked, wondering how she would answer his question.

Cindi's blue eyes looked at something she'd suddenly found interesting over his shoulder. "I'm afraid not. Sam has been unwell for the past several days. I'm not sure when he's coming back to the office."

"Oh, I'm sorry to hear that. Have you spoken to him since he's been out sick?"

She seemed surprised by his question. "Why, uh…no, I haven't." She narrowed her eyes at him. "Why do you ask?"

"Just curious. So when do you expect Mr. Evan Andrews back?"

"Not till tomorrow, but I can have one of our other consultants assist you with financial advice."

"No thanks. I'll stop by tomorrow. It's important I talk to the man in charge…it's kind of a big deal."

"You'll have to make an appointment. He's a very busy man."

"Good to hear. Okay, I'll make an appointment."

She gave him a tight smile. "With Mandy at reception. Have a nice day, sir."

John took the hint and left. He stopped at reception and made arrangements to see Evan Andrews at three the following afternoon. It wasn't as early as he would've liked, but it would have to do. Mandy's smile seemed genuine enough when she gave him a chirpy, "See you tomorrow, Mr. White Eagle."

"Right, see ya."

On his way out of the building, John called Mark. "Hey, you busy?"

"What d'you need?"

"Gotta favor to ask. Can you check your missing persons data and tell me if a Samuel Andrews is on the list?"

"Sure. Give me a few and I'll call you right back."

"Thanks." By the time he'd reached his bike, Mark was calling him back.

"Find anything?"

"Nope, no Samuel Andrews on the missing persons list. There's a Samantha, that's it."

"Interesting."

"This a new case?"

"Yeah, this morning. I'll tell you more when I see you later."

"Okay, take care."

"You too. Bye."

After hanging up, he ducked inside a Starbucks, ordered a hot tea and found an empty table. He unloaded his laptop and googled Samuel Andrews. There were a lot of guys by that name, but he narrowed it down by adding Evan, his father, and Brennan

Financial. A picture of Sam's handsome mug appeared and a link to Wikipedia.

Man, this guy has had a life! The wiki article was long and detailed. Yes, Sam had a position at Brennan Financial, but the more John read, the more it sounded as if the job could most definitely get in the way of what Sam really loved doing. Penny Andrews hadn't been far off the mark when she'd said he was an adventurer. According to the article, he was an environmentalist, an animal rights activist, an explorer… He'd been on archeological digs in Egypt and Peru, and had given lectures at universities. So, these were the things Sam loved to do away from Brennan Financial. The man, if half of this article bore any resemblance to his life, was amazing.

His personal life was sketchier. Married once and divorced within a year. No children. No mention of the ex-wife's name. *Interesting.* Father, Evan Andrews, sibling, Penelope Andrews. Mother deceased. John frowned when he remembered Penny's story about her father blaming her for their mother's death. *What a bastard.*

There were plenty of Sam Andrews on Facebook, but none that jived with the Sam he was looking for, which was a pity. Chatting with a friend or two of his might have thrown some light on his apparent disappearance. Then again, with a resume like his, Sam Andrews could quite literally be anywhere in the world. The only anomaly, at least according to his sister, was that he had chosen to go off without telling a soul where he was going. Or had he, as Penny Andrews feared, been murdered? Perhaps dear old Dad would have some thoughts on the situation, although his lack of caring as to where his son was, or what might have happened to him, did not bode well for any helpful answers.

Of course, that had been Sam's sister's opinion—the man himself might have a completely different version of where his son might be. *Should be interesting.*

* * * *

On his way to meet Mark and Jack, Mark's dad, John stopped in at the local market and purchased a bottle of Dewar's twelve-year-old Scotch, a birthday card that told the lucky recipient he was the best father in all the world, and a *Happy Birthday* balloon. Jack Rossi would no doubt be embarrassed by the balloon, but what the hey? He'd only be sixty-five once.

Mark and Jack were already seated in a booth when he entered Louie's Pub. The big red balloon with a smiley face etched on it caused a stir when the ribbon attached to it slipped through John's fingers as he opened the pub's door, hindered as he was by the wrapped bottle and the card. It sailed around the bar, aided by some of the patrons batting it on its way until one of the bar waitresses in a green uniform caught the ribbon and handed it to John with a smile.

"Who's the lucky birthday guy or gal?" she asked.

"My father-in-law," John told her, returning her smile through his embarrassment. "In the booth over there."

"Oh." She took her time staring at the two men…both of whom were chuckling at John's antics. "Well, I'll be right over to serve the three best-looking men in the place."

"Thanks." He made his way through the crowd to where his husband and father-in-law sat, still chuckling. Mark got up to give him a kiss and grabbed the gift box that contained the bottle of Scotch. "From us, Dad. Happy Birthday."

"Well, thanks, guys." He slipped an arm around John's waist and squeezed while John dropped a kiss on his forehead. With Jack as his father, it was easy to see where Mark had gotten his good looks from. Despite his dark hair now turning gray, he could very easily be mistaken for Mark's older brother.

"Happy birthday to the best father-in-law a guy could ever have," John said, meaning it totally. Jack Rossi was a retired detective sergeant and had been supportive of Mark and John's relationship from the beginning. John handed him the card. "Don't worry," he told Mark. "I signed it from both of us."

Jack opened his card and smiled while reading it. Mark rubbed John's thigh when he sat next to him. "Thanks for doing all that," he whispered in John's ear. "Sorry I sprang it on you this morning."

John shivered at the touch of Mark's lips on his ear as he kissed the lobe. "Not in front of your dad, please."

"Oh, don't mind me." Jack winked. "I'm too old to be shocked by PDA. Better that than yellin' at each other, like some folks I know."

The waitress who had rescued the balloon appeared at their table. "Hi, I'm Anna, and I'll be helping you tonight. What can I get you to drink, birthday boy?"

Jack beamed at her. "Thanks for the 'boy'! I'll have a Guinness, thank you."

"Ah, puts hair on your chest," Anna said. She had an Irish lilt to her voice. "That's why I never drink it."

Jack laughed like it was the funniest thing he'd ever heard. "That's a good one. Now John here could use some hair on his chest."

"Yes, but he has beautiful hair on his head," Anna said. She raised an eyebrow at Mark. "You're a lucky man for sure an' all."

"Yes, I am," Mark agreed. "Uh, we'll both have the Kronenbourg lager."

"Comin' right up." She hurried off toward the bar.

"So, how was your day, John?" Jack asked.

"Interesting. I have a new missing person case."

"Oh yeah," Mark said. "Samuel Andrews. Sorry I couldn't come up with anything."

"That's okay, just makes it more interesting." He waited until Anna had placed their beers in front of them with a flirty, "Drink up, boys," before continuing. After they'd lifted their glasses and wished Jack happy birthday again, both men gazed at him, waiting for him to continue.

"A young lady, Penny Andrews, came to the office this morning. Her brother, Sam, has been missing for over a week and she's under the impression that her father might have killed him…whether by accident or on purpose, she wasn't sure. Sam works at Brennan Financial, where the father's the CEO. I went there to question him, but he wasn't available, according to his secretary, although he could've been lurking behind the office door for all I knew. I have an appointment with him tomorrow afternoon at three."

"Wonder why the sister didn't report him as missing," Mark mused. "If she's concerned enough to hire a private detective, surely her first option would have been to call the police?"

"You'd think so, but she said her father would go ballistic if the police were involved. I'm guessing that he'd consider it bad for business. Then there's the fact that father and son don't get along too well, to put it mildly."

"But that's not a reason to not report your son missing," Jack said, shaking his head. "It's a bit callous. I know that if either of you two went missing, I'd get the police involved immediately."

"Thanks, Jack." John smiled at his father-in-law. He loved the fact that Jack thought of him as his son. "But from what Miss Andrews told me, callous is the least of it."

"What d'you mean?" Mark asked.

"She told me good old Dad blames her for her mother's death. A bad labor he says she never really recovered from. He throws that at her, apparently, when he's mad about something or other."

"Shit," Mark muttered. "He sounds like a real winner."

"He sounds like a man with no conscience or compassion," Jack added.

"But does he sound like a man who'd kill his own son?" John shrugged. "I'll reserve that opinion until I meet with him tomorrow."

* * * *

John and Mark arrived home almost at the same time. John had kept pace on his bike with Mark's Altima. "Hope Jack had a good time," John remarked as he closed the garage door then entered the house behind Mark.

Mark turned and kissed John's cheek. "He did…even said he liked the balloon. Hopes it won't deflate too fast."

"He is a sweetheart."

Mark chuckled. "Don't call him that in front of his buddies. He likes to maintain his bad-ass rep from when he was with the force. Some of them are taking him out tomorrow night, by the way. We're invited, if you want to go."

"What d'you think?"

"I think it might be nice for him to let his hair down without his son and son-in-law watching his alcohol intake. He promised he'd Uber home."

"You're right, as long as he's safe."

"Are you ready for bed, or d'you want a nightcap?"

"No more firewater for me, Kemo Sabe. You know what it does to us redskins." Mark used to flinch when John used derogatory terms for his race, until John had told him, with a cheeky grin, that it wasn't racist when he said it.

"I'm banking on it," Mark said now with a salacious wink.

John chuckled. "You know you don't need to get me drunk to have your way with me. I'm all yours, body and soul. But right now, this body needs a shower."

"That sounds like fun too."

"Thought you'd think so." He took Mark's hand and led him into the bedroom. They'd known the house needed some fixing when they'd bought it, and their priorities, after painting all the walls inside and out, had been installing new floors, a mixture of wood and carpet. Then they'd splurged on a new tub and walk-in shower in the master bathroom.

"Room for two to get frisky in," had been Mark's assessment, and John had lost track of how many times they'd fulfilled that particular desire. It seemed that when they were naked, and quite often when fully

clothed, even after ten years together, desire was still the name of the game.

John ogled Mark's tan body as he stripped off. They'd gone on a trip to Hawaii the month before. A full week of nothing but relaxation, swimming and surfing to their hearts' content. They'd both soaked up the sun and Mark's normally olive skin had deepened to a dark brown. His tan line made his ass appear pale in contrast and, in John's mind, even more defined, more delicious.

Mark turned on the shower spray, stepped inside then held out his hand for John to join him. Once under the hot spray, they kissed and embraced before smoothing body shampoo over each other's skin. Mark ran his soapy hands under John's armpits then slid them around and down John's spine, trailing his fingers into John's crack. He palmed the cheeks apart and slid one finger inside John.

"God, but I love your sweet butt," he whispered.

"And it's yours for the taking," John whispered back.

"You're so easy," Mark teased him.

"Only for you, lover."

"Mmm..." Mark trailed his lips over John's, parting them with the tip of his tongue, which John eagerly sucked into his mouth. No matter how many times they had kissed, probably thousands over their years together, Mark never failed to ignite a spark in John's blood every time they kissed like this. Ten years down the road, John was still as much in lust as he was in love with his husband.

He moaned into Mark's mouth, gripped Mark's butt with both hands and pulled him even closer, grinding their hard cocks together. Soap bubbles gathered between their meshed torsos, letting them slip and slide over each other, the sensual contact enough for John to start losing control. He broke the kiss and eased back a little to rein himself in.

"Whoa," he panted. "Don't want this to be over so quick." Even after all the years of living and loving together, Mark's kisses and the sensation of his bare skin pressed sensually against John's could bring him effortlessly to the brink of climax. "Want you inside me when I come."

"We can do that." Mark turned off the faucet and handed a towel to John, who ran it rapidly over his hair. While still damp, it fell in the lush blue-black waves down his back that Mark had said so often he loved to kiss and run his hands through, which he now did. "Like silk," he murmured, steering John out of the bathroom.

John willingly let himself be guided backward until his thighs touched the bed and he fell onto the comforter, taking Mark with him, their naked bodies rolling across the silky material in a tangle of arms and legs. John squirmed around enough to get his face between Mark's legs so he could blow him. He loved the feel and taste of Mark's hard cock, the salty tang of his pre-cum as Mark slid his erection into John's mouth. He sucked on the pulsing flesh long and hard, relishing not only the sensation of the hot, rigid length between his lips but also the soft moans and gasps that came from Mark as he arched his hips, giving John even more to suck on.

"John… *God*, John." Mark's breathing was labored. "John, if you want me to fuck you, you better stop what you're doing. Jeez, never thought I'd ever say that, but…"

John released him and spread his body over Mark's, taking his mouth in one hot kiss after another. He smiled against Mark's lips. "Your wish and all that..." He sat up and reached for the lube, then looked down into Mark's slightly glazed blue eyes as he slicked himself then Mark's rock-hard erection. Mark ran his hands up John's torso, teasing both nipples while John impaled himself on Mark's prodigious length.

"Oh, yeah..." He exhaled a long breath as Mark slid all the way inside him. "So good, Mark. Love you so much. Never get enough of you..." He claimed Mark's lips again to kiss through their incredible fuck as Mark used his muscular strength to ram hard inside John, gasping into John's mouth, telling him how much he was loved.

John arched his body in rapture, leaning back, supporting himself with a hand on either side of Mark's thighs as Mark drove into him with long, hard thrusts.

"Love you too," Mark murmured. "Always will..." His body shuddered from the growing heat at the base of his spine. "John, I'm coming...gonna come so hard..."

John reared up and yelled as he let his orgasm take him, jetting his creamy cum over his and Mark's chests at the same time as Mark climaxed and shot deep inside him. He collapsed over Mark, raining kisses over his face and throat, whispering *mahasani*, the Sioux word for lover, and some words even he didn't understand but that felt good and right in the moment.

"John, John..." Mark murmured in his ear. "You still have that voodoo thing, or were we really flying?"

John chuckled and kissed Mark's chest. "What do you think?"

"I think it's that voodoo that you do so well."

John laughed softly and caressed Mark's face. "It isn't voodoo or witchcraft. I used to believe the story my grandmother told me about having the power to raise someone's ecstasy to heights they had never known before. Maybe it seemed so because I was young and any sex I had felt terrific. Maybe it was just easy for me to make the other guy believe it too. But with you and me, it's simply love, and the fact that we fit together so well."

"You're right." Mark kissed John's chin. "We do fit together well and have done for all the years we've been together. But now, *mahasani,* we have to get up and get clean. Sounds like another shower's in our future."

John beamed at him. "You mean we get to do it all over again?"

"What gave you that idea?"

"You, me, naked, shower. All elements that usually lead to one thing."

Mark sighed. "I married a sex machine."

"For which you will thank the gods over and over." John poked him in the ribs. "I mean, I hear you calling to them every time we have sex. Oh God, John…Jesus, John…Oh my God, J— Ow!"

"That slap on your butt is one of many if you keep that up." Mark gave him an evil grin. "Just for that, it's a shower, and only a shower." He rolled off the bed. "Coming?"

John chuckled. "Not till after the shower."

Chapter Three

Over coffee the following morning, John told Mark what he'd discovered about Sam Andrews. "The guy would be pretty amazing with just half of those accomplishments under his belt."

Mark nodded. "He doesn't sound like someone who'd just up and leave without a word. Although, as we both know, people can do the strangest things at times. Maybe the pressure of being a part of so many ventures got to him, and he just needed to get away for a time without anyone knowing where he was. A kind of sabbatical?"

"It's possible." John mulled over Mark's words. "But why not at least tell his sister what he was doing? She says they're very close. Surely he'd know she'd be worried at his lack of contact."

"*If* they're as close as she says they are." Mark frowned. "From what you've told me, something about the family dynamics makes me think she might be wrong about that. The father and son hate each other, the father blames his daughter for his wife's death and the daughter was ready to throw her father under the bus for his son's disappearance. Even going so far as to accuse him of the son's death—and at the moment we don't even know whether he's deceased or not."

John shook his head. "Yeah, happy families doesn't come close to what they are." He sighed. "Well, the meeting with the father should be interesting."

"About that, John..." Mark took his hand. "Be careful when you talk to Andrews. If he is somehow involved in Sam Andrews' disappearance, he might just make some kind of foolish move."

"I can handle it, but..." He squeezed Mark's hand in response. "I will be careful, I promise."

"Let me know how it went soon as you leave his office."

"I will."

* * * *

Millie looked her usual pleased self when John showed up at his office later that morning. "A gentleman who says he knows you called, John. From, and I quote, your wild west days."

"Oh, yeah? Did he leave a name?"

"Alexandro Vasquez...very exotic, I must say."

"Oh, Alex. He and I were film extras back in the day. We worked on a couple of movies together, including the one I told you about where the star, Greg Mathis, tried to frame me for murder. Alex and I were both bad Injuns and got what was coming to us. I think I was better at pretend dying than he was." He chuckled, remembering. "Did he say what he wanted?"

"Just to see you. I said you were free at ten this morning." She glanced at her computer screen before continuing, "I hope that's all right. I did check your schedule and the only appointment you have is with Mr. Andrews at three."

"That's cool. It'll be good to see him again. We weren't the closest of friends, but we shared some good times and laughs with the other extras when we'd get together for a drink. Then one day he said he was moving to Chicago, and I never heard from him again."

"Well, he sounded eager to see you again. Would you care for some coffee?"

"Yes, please."

"I'll bring it through."

"Thanks, Millie."

He wandered off into his office and pulled up Sam Andrews' information again. According to the wiki article, which was more up to date than many of them, he'd been lecturing at a UCI campus earlier in the month and had another scheduled for next month at the Irvine campus. The article made a point of saying that his lectures were usually standing room only, so anyone interested should call ahead to avoid missing out. He looked up the number for UCI and asked who he could talk to about a past and future speaker named Samuel Andrews.

A sweet-voiced woman said that would be Coral Browne and she could put him right through. "Thank you, you've been very helpful," he told her.

Coral Browne was also helpful, telling him that Mr. Andrews was indeed scheduled to speak in three weeks' time, and no, she had not had any word of him canceling. "I sincerely hope not, as his lectures are always so popular and people would be so disappointed if we had to postpone or cancel."

"How did Mr. Andrews seem on his last visit?"

"Oh, excellent." Miss Browne was a tad gushy. "He's such a fine young man, and his wealth of experience makes his lectures so interesting. The young people love him because he's a true humanitarian and cares for our planet's future. We always look forward to his visits." She paused for a moment then said, "May I ask why you're inquiring?"

"Well, Mr. Andrews has kinda disappeared."

"Oh, no!"

"'Fraid so. His sister came to see me yesterday and asked if I'd find out what's happened to him. I'm a private investigator. Name's John White Eagle."

"Oh…an unusual name."

"Not if you're a Native American."

"Oh, no…I suppose not. Well, I'm sure Mr. Andrews will be in touch before long. Have you met him? I'm sure you'd get along just fine with him. He's also an advocate for the indigenous peoples' welfare. A private investigator…I'm sure he'd find that very interesting."

John forced down the chuckle that had almost sprung from his throat. "Well, hopefully I'll get a chance to meet and talk with him. If you should by any chance hear from him about anything at all, please call me." He recited his cell number then hung up. He smiled as Millie brought in his mug of fresh coffee.

"Thank you, lifesaver. I've got some notes for you to enter in the computer. Penny Andrews' brother is scheduled to appear at UCI next month and there's been no word of him canceling the engagement."

"If he's been *detained* somewhere, he might not be in any condition to cancel anything," Millie said dryly.

"True. I have an appointment with the father at three this afternoon, so maybe he'll throw some light on his son's whereabouts."

"Especially if he's killed the poor boy."

John grinned. "You have ears like a bat, even with the door closed. Guess I better be careful when I'm on the phone with Mark."

Millie gave him a haughty look. "I would never eavesdrop on your conversations with *Mark*. I simply pay attention to what your clients are telling you in case you miss or forget something later."

"Ah, Millie. I don't know what I'd do without you."

"As long as you appreciate it, I am content. Now, what about the Andrews girl? Is she on the level, do you think?"

John blinked. "You think she might not be?"

"Well, it is a bit outlandish, isn't it? Telling you her father did the brother in."

"It's happened before. Murder among families isn't that unusual. I have to admit, I was a bit surprised when she came close to accusing her dad of the deed, but I talked it over with Mark and he agreed—stranger things than that have happened."

"I suppose so. I shouldn't be surprised either. The news is full of terrible goings-on, but I don't know… I suppose I'm just a cynic at heart." The sound of the door opening interrupted their conversation. "That'll be Mr. Vasquez. I'll send him through."

John smiled, listening to Millie greet Alex with a cheerfulness not many receptionists could match. A moment later, she shepherded him into John's office.

"Mr. Vasquez," Millie announced.

"Hey, Alex." John stood to welcome his friend. They traded hugs, then Alex sat opposite John. "You look good," John told him. And he did. The epitome of tall, dark and handsome, and fit—the tight white T-shirt that covered his muscular torso was the proof of that. "What've you been up to?"

Alex gave him a tight-lipped smile. "Things have been okay until recently. I keep tryin' to stay outta trouble, but it has a habit of finding me, regardless."

John frowned. "What kind of trouble?"

"Well, this time it's some jerk who wants to put me in jail."

"In jail for what?"

Alex hunched his shoulders and sank farther back into the chair. "He *says* I beat him up when I asked him for the money he owed me after we had sex."

John stared at him with wide eyes. "You're in the escort business?"

He nodded. "Have to make a buck now that the studios don't seem to like me anymore. Haven't had a decent offer in over a year."

John sat back in his chair and gazed at his friend with sympathy. "What's going on, Alex?"

The question seemed to sap Alex's strength. His shoulders slumped and he looked at a spot on the wall behind John's head. "So, you know how the film business is. There's too many of us wannabes and the jobs get fewer and fewer. I'm tired of calling do-nothin' agents who don't ever call you back. Tired of standing around at cattle-calls they say are auditions, just to find they only want two or three out of the hundred or so guys there—some of 'em younger and better-lookin' than me. Just tired, John, is all."

"I don't envy you. I'm glad to say I never got to that stage in my career," John told him. "The extra work kinda lost its edge for me. I got a shot at a series, but it got canceled after two episodes. Mark wanted me to join the force, but they said I'd have to cut my hair, and no way was I going to do that."

"What...you thought it might sap your strength, like Samson?"

John chuckled. "No, smarty. It's a tribal tradition."

Alex snorted. "Right."

"Well, okay, I just like keeping it long, and Mark likes it too. Anyway, when I told Mark I was over the uncertainty of film extra work and wanted to do something more meaningful, he suggested I study for a private detective license, and here I am."

"Good for you. I never had much of an education, so taking exams and such would just be a waste of time. Escorting isn't so bad. I'm still in shape and some guys like the more mature type. Long as it comes with a big dick." He smiled smugly. "Anyway, this guy who says I beat him up is lying. I've never come on strong with any of my clients, even the ones who like to take a walk on the rough side. I'm always careful not to leave bruises, and always insist on a safe word."

"So tell me how this guy approached you."

"I run an ad in a couple of the gay mags. He called for a hook-up. I told him what my fee was, and he said he had plenty of money, so no problem. I must've dozed off after we had sex, and when I woke up, he was gone, and no money left behind. Then he called me again the day after. Of course, I remembered him because he'd stiffed me and I, dumbass that I am, thought he was calling to say, 'Hey sorry 'bout not payin' you, will you take a check?'—or something like that, anyway. But no, he was screaming that I'd beaten the shit outta him, and he had the marks to prove it and was goin' to the cops if I didn't shell out ten grand."

"So, blackmail..."

"There's more. I told him he was crazy, that I hadn't laid a hand on him even though he'd really pissed me off—and, need I add, he was a lousy lay?" Alex rolled his eyes. "Jeez, the worst. I had to use every trick in the book to make him come. The fucker wore me out—

that's most likely why I fell asleep after. And furthermore, I told him he was even crazier to think I had ten grand laying around to pay off fuckin' blackmailing sons of bitches like him. He went berserk, callin' me names, some I'd never heard before. He ended up by tellin' me that if I didn't cough up the money, he'd go to the cops with the proof of my beating on him, and give them my online profile that would put me away for solicitation, as well as the bruises I'd left on him."

"Hmm…" Alex's story sounded legit enough, John thought. "Sounds like he thinks you'll cave rather than have a police record. Could be he's tried this before on other guys in the business and maybe had some luck with it. How are you supposed to get in touch with him to give him the money?"

"He left a cell number…but I am not paying him, John. Even if I had ten grand, which I don't, he's not gonna see a penny of it."

"Right, and the cell's most likely a burner, but we need to meet with him, scare the shit outta him and find out how many other guys he's done this to."

"Oh, okay. I'm good with that." Alex balled up his fists.

"No violence, Alex," John warned him. "We need to scare him, not smack him around. What kind of guy is he? Young, old?"

"Not real old…maybe in his late thirties, out of shape, and like I said…a lousy lay."

"Well, we can't use being a lousy lay against him. Only the blackmail, and if he's running some kind of scam and tried to con some other guys too." John drummed his fingers on his desktop. "Okay, call him, set up a time and place and let me know where and when. I have a three o'clock, but any time after that will be good."

"Thanks, John." Alex stood, ready to go. "Uh, what will I owe you for this? I know you guys don't work for nothing."

"We'll talk about that later. Just call me after you've spoken to whatshisname."

"Shit, that's right." Alex frowned. "I don't remember the guy's name, even. Guess I'll find out when I call him."

* * * *

Mandy wasn't at her post when John arrived for his appointment with Evan Andrews. Instead, a young man with a blond buzzcut stared at John through sleepy eyes. He wasn't wearing a name tag on his Versace-inspired shirt. So many vivid colors almost hurt John's eyes.

"Can I help you?"

"I'm here to see Mr. Andrews. I have a three o'clock."

"Just a sec." He punched a key on his computer. "Oh yeah, Mr. John White Eagle. Cool name."

"Thanks."

"I'll take you through to Cindi's office. I think Mr. Andrews had a two-thirty, so he might be running late." John nodded and followed the male receptionist past the lines of cubicles and the stares of the employees.

Cindi rose to meet him with another of her searching looks. Today she was wearing a white pantsuit, the jacket open to expose her cleavage. "Mr. White Eagle, good to see you again. Mr. Andrews will be with you momentarily."

"Thanks."

The nameless receptionist left after giving John a thumbs up. Cindi gestured toward a couple of armchairs. "Make yourself comfortable, Mr. White Eagle. Would you like some tea or coffee?"

"No thanks. Have you heard from Sam today?"

Cindi startled. "Sam? No, why should I? Do you know him?"

"I know his sister, Penny. She's the one who said I should talk to her father."

"Oh yes? You're a friend of hers?"

"Kind of…" He stood as the door to the inner office opened and two men exited. One, he recognized as Evan Andrews from the photo he'd googled.

"Cindi, make another appointment for Mr. Colburn for next week." He shook hands with Colburn then glanced at John.

"This is Mr. White Eagle, your three o'clock, Mr. Andrews," Cindi said before leading the other client over to her desk

"Mr. White Eagle…" Andrews eyed John up and down then asked, "How can I help you?"

"Maybe we should talk in your office. It's kinda personal."

"Very well." He strode inside his office, obviously expecting John to follow, which he did. "What can I help you with? Cindi said you needed some financial advice."

"Actually, I don't need that kind of advice. I'm here because your daughter Penny asked me to find her brother Sam, and as you're the head of the clan, I figured if anyone knows where he is, it'd be you. So, do you know where your son is, Mr. Andrews?"

"Who the hell are you?"

"We've been introduced, Mr. Andrews. John White Eagle, private detective, working on behalf of your daughter, Miss Penny Andrews."

Andrews gave John a narrow-eyed look and grimaced. "That foolish girl, involving you in this purely family matter. No, I don't know where he is. Knowing Sam, he's probably on one of his digs in…just about anywhere. Or he's out there trying to save the environment, if not the whole damn world. He doesn't tell me where he's going, and frankly, I don't care."

"Really? Hardly a paternal sentiment, Mr. Andrews." John frowned. "Your daughter seems to think he's been involved in some kind of violent accident…or perhaps not so accidental. Does that not concern you?"

Andrews' face flushed a deep red. "What kind of bullshit is this? I'll talk to Penny and put her straight about talking to strangers about family affairs."

"What does that mean—put her straight? Are you a violent man, Mr. Andrews? Penny tells me you have a temper and that you and your son are prone to violent arguments."

"Get out!"

John narrowed his eyes. "Seems she's right about the temper. Just so you know, I've checked with the LAPD and there's no report of a Sam Andrews listed as a missing person. He's been gone for over a week. Your secretary told me he'd called out sick. Is he sick, Mr. Andrews? In the hospital perhaps? But Penny would know about that, wouldn't she? Just where is he?"

"I told you I don't know where he is," Andrews seethed. "Now get out of my office—and stay away from my daughter."

"Can't do that, I'm afraid, Mr. Andrews. I'm under her employ, so to speak."

"How much do you want?" Andrews rasped.

"For what?"

"To go away and stop sticking your fucking nose in affairs that don't concern you."

John sighed. "Mr. Andrews, I just got done telling you that your daughter employed me to find her brother. She is very concerned for his safety, and I intend to find out what happened to him, or at least where he is, so I can put her mind at ease. I'm a private detective, this is what I do and your attempt to buy me off just increases my suspicion that somehow you are involved in this situation."

"There is no *situation*," Andrews hissed. "Now get the fuck out of here, before I call the police."

"Perhaps you should, and while you're at it, report that your son is missing."

"He's not missing, he's—"

"Dead?"

"No, you cretin. He's not dead. Jesus Christ!" Andrews looked as if he might implode at any moment.

"All right, Mr. Andrews, that's the good news. Don't you think you could've told your daughter what you obviously know, before she felt bound to come to me about this? So, where is he?"

"I told you I don't know." For a moment, Andrews appeared almost nervous. "Like I said before, he could be anywhere."

"Then how do you know he's still alive?"

"I heard from him three days ago."

John snorted with exasperation. "And you couldn't tell your daughter that?"

"The less she knows, the better," Andrews snapped. "He's got himself mixed up in some stupidity she's better off not knowing about."

"Ah, the old cliché. But think on this—it would stop her worrying about him, at the very least." John shrugged. "If, as you say, he's involved in some *stupidity,* then that's his business, I guess. Okay, I'll make my report to her that he's alive, whereabouts unknown. If he calls again, tell him to call his sister soon as he can…if he cares about her wellbeing at all. Have a nice day."

John turned from Andrews and headed for the door. He gave Cindi a cursory wave on the way out. He really hoped he didn't have to come talk to Andrews again. The guy gave him the creeps…and what possible reason could he have for not letting Penny know her brother was in fact okay? Or was he lying through his teeth about hearing from his son in the last few days? "*Some stupidity he was mixed up in,*" he'd said. Would Penny Andrews know anything about that?

He punched in the number he'd programmed into his phone. Penny answered on the first ring. "Yeah, hi, Miss Andrews, it's John White Eagle. Do you live with your dad?"

"No, thank heavens," she said gasping slightly. "I have my own place."

"Good, that's a relief, 'cause I kinda threw you under the bus, so it might be good to stay out of his way for a couple of days."

"What d'you mean?"

"I mentioned you'd said he had a temper and that he and Sam got into some violent arguments at times. He wasn't happy, but he did say he'd heard from your brother recently and that he's not, in fact, missing. I asked why he hadn't told you that and his excuse was a lame 'better she doesn't know' kind of thing."

"No, no…Sam wouldn't call him and not me."

"You're sure of that?"

"Absolutely. I told you we are very close. Sam hated our father, so unless there was something really bad going on, he'd never call him…never."

"He said Sam had got himself mixed up in some kind of stupidity. Any idea what that might be?"

She was silent for several seconds before mumbling, "No, I have no idea."

"Hmm…okay, let me do some more digging. I kinda thought your father was lying to me just to get me out of his office. Does Sam have any close friends…like, who he would've told if he was going to be out of town for a few days?"

"I really don't know any of his friends." She sounded clearer now. "Oh, apart from Dave…Dave Richards. But I called him already and he said he hadn't heard from Sam for a couple of weeks."

"So, not really close, *close* friends then. How about his ex-wife?"

"I doubt it. They weren't exactly on the greatest terms when they divorced. I haven't heard from her in…oh, two or three years. I think she remarried, but I'm not sure."

John sighed. So many dead ends. If Sam Andrews wanted to disappear, it looked as if he'd have very little trouble accomplishing just that. "Okay," he said, fishing his notepad from his pocket. "D'you have Dave Richards' number? I'll call him just in case I can jog his memory."

"Sure, just a sec. I'm afraid I don't have Sonia's number…that's his ex. Here's Dave's." She recited the number and John entered it into his notepad.

"I'll call you later, hopefully with better news. Take care, Miss Andrews." John disconnected the call, puzzling over her reluctance to answer when he'd quoted what her father had said about Sam getting mixed up in some kind of stupidity. Did she actually know what that might have meant and didn't want to acknowledge it? *Man, but this family has problems!*

Chapter Four

As he walked to the parking garage to collect his bike, he called Dave Richards, but that went to voicemail so he left his name and cell number along with a brief message saying that her was a friend of Penny Andrews and would like to talk to him. He called Alex for an update, but he said he hadn't heard back yet from his blackmailer.

His cell buzzed as he pulled into his office building's parking lot. *Mark… Shit, I was supposed to call him soon as I left Evan Andrews' office.*

He pulled off his helmet. "Hi, handsome."

"John, you were supposed to call me, remember?"

"Yeah, sorry, I got into a conversation with the sister that left me with more questions than answers."

"That's how it goes sometimes. Anyway, everything okay? How did it go with Andrews?"

"I get the feeling the guy's hiding something," John replied as he climbed the steps leading to his office. "One minute he doesn't know where his son is—and doesn't care—next he's telling me he spoke to him three days ago. He's either lying or his daughter is right about what happened to her brother."

"Andrews killed his son, you mean."

"Yeah..." John pushed the office door open and gave Millie a thumb's-up as he passed her desk. "But that doesn't sound right either. I didn't get a killer vibe from the old man...he seemed kinda weak to me. Full of bluster, but weak. He tried to pay me off, then told me to get the fuck out of his office. I dunno. I have the number of a friend of Sam's, so I might get something there."

"I might be late getting home," Mark said, "so don't wait dinner. I have a meeting with the brass that I can't get out of. It could last a few hours."

"Okay. Oh, by the way, Alex Vasquez came to see me at the office."

"Oh, yeah? How's he doing?"

"He's being blackmailed, so he asked me to help him out and—"

"Shit, sorry, John. I have to go. I'll call you later. Stay safe."

"Right, love you..." But the connection was broken before Mark could reply, or perhaps before he heard the words.

"Everything all right?" Millie called out.

"Oh, yeah." He changed his mind about sitting down and strolled over to where Millie was busy on her computer. "Mark's gonna be late home...some kind of meeting, he said."

"Was Mr. Andrews of help to you?"

"I wouldn't say that, but he did insist that his son isn't missing and that he spoke to him three days ago."

"Then why does Miss Andrews think he's missing?"

"Because dear Dad didn't tell her he'd heard from his son. Also, she's convinced that her brother would've called her, not their father. She more or less said he was lying."

"Quite the conundrum."

John chuckled. "Not a word I'd use, but I guess it fits. Think I'll do some more research on Sam Andrews' background…see if something clicks."

"I'll make you some fresh coffee."

"Thanks, Millie."

Back at his desk, he fired up his computer and signed on to the app that gave him a more detailed account of whoever he was researching. At first, after he'd entered Andrews' name, it was more or less what he'd seen on the Google site, but with one difference. There was a gap of six months and no record of his whereabouts during that time just before his divorce in 2017.

Wonder where he was for six months? He picked up his cell and punched in Penny Andrews' number.

"Hi again," he said when she answered. "It's John White Eagle."

"Oh, hello. Do you have some news?"

"I have a question. Do you remember where your brother might have been for six months in 2017?"

There was a long pause before she stammered, "T-two thousand and what?"

"Seventeen. I'm doing a background check on him, and just before his divorce, there's no record of where he might've been from February through July of that year."

"Oh, let me think. Oh yes, he was with a civilian peacekeeping group in Afghanistan. It was kind of hush-hush, so that would account for there being no record of it, I suppose."

John thanked her then disconnected the call. Her explanation sounded okay. From what he'd learned of Sam Andrews, he did seem the type to take on a peacekeeping mission. He had to admit that meeting Andrews would be something he'd enjoy. *Hope he's not dead...* Millie arrived with his coffee. "How do you manage to make this so delicious? Darned if I can get that same flavor at home—and it's the exact same brand."

"It's the enchantment spell I mutter over it as it brews," Millie said with a straight face.

"Ha! Good one. Well, it works. You'll have to write it down so I can surprise Mark with a decent cup of coffee."

They were both chuckling when John's cell buzzed. He glanced at the screen. "Alex...I better take this. Hey, Alex. Any news?"

"Yeah, the fucker wants to meet me at eight tonight, and I better have the money, he said. Well, I'm meeting him all right, without the money, of course. Like I have ten grand in my pocket."

"I better go with you, Alex," John said quickly.

"I can handle him."

"Probably, but what if he's armed, or got a bunch of heavies with him?"

Alex chuckled. "He's not the kinda guy who knows any heavies."

"You don't know that, Alex. Where are you meeting him?"

"Jericho Park. He said there's a bench near the entrance where he'll be waiting. But honestly, John, does he really believe I'm just going to hand over ten thousand dollars? He has to be some kind of nutcase."

"Did you get his name this time?"

"No."

John sighed. "Too bad. I could've run a check on him, see if he has a record for extortion…or any kind of record. Anyway, I'm going to the park with you. Mark's working late so I don't have to come up with an excuse as to why I'm not home."

"Okay, if you think it's best."

"I do. The guy's already a blackmailer. You don't know what else kinda shit he might pull. Safety in numbers and all that."

"All right. I'll see you at eight."

John hung up and took a sip of his coffee. He had a few hours till eight, time he could use to do some more research on Sam Andrews. For some reason, he thought the missing six months of the man's life was important. "*A civilian peacekeeping group,*" his sister had said. Maybe someone who'd also been on that mission might remember something about him.

"You will be careful tonight, won't you?" Millie's voice from the outer office made him smile.

"Of course I will. When am I not careful?"

"I won't start recounting the list you know so very well," was Millie's tart reply. "But you might want to let Mark know where you'll be, just in case."

"He's got an important meeting, and I don't want to add any pressure to his day. I'll call him after Alex and I have dealt with the blackmailer…whoever the heck he is."

"Very well, but please, John, be careful." Millie gathered up her things. "I'll bid you goodnight, then. See you tomorrow."

"Thanks, Millie. See ya...and yes, I'll be careful."

Millie sniffed. "See that you are."

The door closed quietly behind her. John shook his head and googled *civilian peacekeeping groups*. He quickly found out that most civilians were volunteers and worked under the auspices of the UN and the EU. There were several articles for him to read and he noticed that one name kept cropping up as an advisor or contributor to the articles...Ellis Watkins. A photograph showed an older man with gray hair and a smiling expression. Researching Watkins was a walk in the park. The man was a fan of social media and had Facebook, Twitter and LinkedIn accounts.

He was fifty-nine years old, lived in Long Beach, was a professor at the university there, and had over three thousand FB friends. His latest post announced that he and his wife were camping somewhere out in the desert near Joshua Tree National Park and would be back in town on Friday. John called four-one-one and asked for the residential number for Ellis Watkins. The man might very well have some information pertaining to Sam Andrews' time as a peacekeeper...they might even have worked together. At the very least, it was a step in the right direction. He called the number and left a message asking politely if Mr. Watkins would return his call pertaining to a colleague of his.

Dave Richards called him just after six. At first sounding wary when John introduced himself as a private detective, he warmed a little after John explained he was working for Penny Andrews.

"Is she all right?" The concern in his voice made John think that perhaps Dave had a fondness for the young woman.

"Yes, she's worried about her brother Sam's disappearance. She mentioned she'd called you about that."

"Oh, yeah, but she shouldn't worry about Sam... He's forever galivanting off on some quest or other. The man's a born nomad. She'll hear from him eventually, I'm sure of it."

"Do you know of any other friends he might have?"

"Not really. He talks about so-and-so at times, but Sam's a bit of a lone wolf. Not the most social guy. He holds a lot of himself close to his chest, as it were. We can go weeks without seeing each other, but that's okay, really."

There wasn't much more Richards knew of Sam's disappearance, so John let him go with his thanks. *Maybe Ellis Watkins will have more information when I can get a hold of him. If the guy isn't dead then someone must know where he is.*

* * * *

On his way to meet Alex, John started to get a cramping feeling in the pit of his stomach. He hated when that happened. It generally signaled something was wrong, that he was heading into a situation that could go sideways. Meeting a man intent on blackmail might not have been the brightest idea for Alex to agree to. He had no intention of paying the guy, so there was bound to be some kind of fallout when Alex told him that. He could only hope that neither man was armed. He didn't think Alex would pull a gun, but what did he really know about him? They hadn't been in touch for a long time, and Alex's new profession could have led him into contact with some shady characters. For example, the blackmailer…

Shit. The discomfort in his stomach became more noticeable the nearer he got to his destination. *Man, I just know this is not what I want to be doing right now…*

The sun was setting as John pulled his Harley into a parking bay near Jericho Park. The trees cast long shadows on the ground as he walked quickly to the park entrance. In the dimming light it was hard to make out anyone at first, but then he spotted Alex. He was staring down at a prone figure. *What the…?*

He raced through the gate. "What happened?"

"I don't know." Alex's voice held a tremor as he dragged his gaze from the body back to John. He was lying there when I arrived."

John knelt by the body and checked for a pulse. There wasn't one. The man was dead. Maybe the knife stuck between his shoulder blades had something to do with it. He glanced up at Alex. "You see anyone else around when you got here?"

Alex shook his head. He looked as if he'd been smacked with a baseball bat. His shock seemed real enough, which gave John a sense of relief. "You didn't touch anything, did you?" he asked. "Like the knife handle."

"No, no way would I touch anything…especially that knife. Jesus."

John nodded, pulled out his cell and punched in Mark's number. A woman's scream behind them made him jump. "*Shit…*yeah, sorry, Mark. The guy Alex and I were meeting is dead. He's been stabbed in the back. The knife's still there."

"Be right there. Jericho Park, right?"

"Yeah." He stood and glared at the woman who'd screamed. The man with her gave John a pugnacious scowl.

"You do this?" he growled.

John sighed. "Sure, then I called the cops and now I'm waiting for them to show up so they can arrest me. Of course I didn't do it, and neither did he." He flicked his thumb in Alex's direction then stared at the spot where Alex had been standing. "Son of a bitch…" Alex had gone.

"He took off," the woman said, "when you were on your phone." She seemed fixated on the sight of the dead man, even taking a step forward until the man with her grabbed her arm to stop her. "Who is he?"

"That we won't know until the police identify him. They should be here any minute."

"Who are you, anyway?" The man's belligerent attitude hadn't dissipated.

"Name's John. I'm a private detective."

"You don't look like one. What's with the long hair?"

"Don't be rude, Harry." The woman pulled her arm free of Harry's hold. "He has lovely hair."

John sent up a silent prayer that Mark and the police would show up in a matter of minutes. These people were weirding him out. And Alex taking off like that… *What the actual fuck was he thinking? Surely he knows that running from the scene of a crime is gonna look bad for him.* And now, when he thought about it, what if Alex had killed the guy and was only acting all shook up? He hadn't pegged Alex for the violent type, but it was obvious life hadn't been easy for him recently, and faced with blackmail, people sometimes did crazy things. *Best thing to do is ask...* He punched in the number Alex had given him. It went to voicemail.

"Alex, what the heck are you doing? Where are you? Call me soon as you can."

He sighed with relief when he heard the blare of a police siren and a couple of black and whites, along with an ambulance, pulled up at the entrance to the park. Two cops, both big and burly, hands on their guns and intimidating as hell, strode toward him. The woman squeaked and stepped behind Harry.

For a moment, John thought they were about to arrest him, or worse, then one of them barked, "You John White Eagle?"

John nodded. "Yes."

"Detective Sergeant Rossi is right behind us. He said to make sure you were okay."

"I am. This couple can give you statements. I'm not sure how much they saw of the incident, but—"

"All we saw was you kneeling over the body," Harry said. "The other guy with you ran when you called the cops."

"Other man?" one of the cops asked.

John sighed. "Yeah...Alex Vasquez. He told me the dead guy was blackmailing him and I offered to come here with him to meet the guy and work something out. When I got here, Alex was standing looking down at the body. He said he hadn't touched anything. Why he ran, I have no idea."

Mark arrived at that moment, accompanied by two men John recognized as Stan Crowley, the city coroner, and his assistant, Brett Chambers.

"Where's Alex?" Mark asked.

"He took off when I called you." John shrugged. "Don't ask me why. I left him a message on his cell. Told him to call me soon as he can."

Mark directed the officers to take statements from the couple then walked over to where Stan was kneeling by the body.

"Interesting. Whoever did this left the knife behind," Stan remarked.

"He might've had to leave in a hurry," Mark said.

Stan nodded. "Nice one too. Indian, from the looks of the intricate carving on the handle. Severed the spinal cord, looks like. Let's turn him over, Brett."

John stepped nearer to see just who had been blackmailing Alex. The man was youngish—early thirties, John figured. His face was slack, and his eyes and mouth were open as if he had been about to say something when he'd been struck down from behind. Stan slipped a hand inside the man's leather jacket and handed Mark a billfold.

Mark opened it and stared at the driver's license. "Donald Forsythe. D.O.B. ten twelve nineteen eighty-four. Nevada license." He turned to John. "We need to find Alex."

Chapter Five

"Donald Forsythe has a record. A DUI, theft...six months in the county jail for that, and he spent two years in prison for, guess what? Blackmailing. So, lesson not learned." Mark sat back from his computer and turned to face John. They were ensconced in Mark's office, a small space off the precinct's bullpen. Through the window, John could see that there was a shift change going on, detectives coming and going, shooting the breeze with one another, or trading information. "So it looks pretty certain that he was the one blackmailing Alex. But what made that idiot run?"

"My call to you would be my guess." John rested his ass on the edge of Mark's desk. "He told me that he's been escorting. That's how he encountered Forsythe. According to Alex, the guy stiffed him then said Alex threatened to beat him up. Alex denies the beating-up threat, said it never happened and that Forsythe was a real jerk."

"Forsythe was married and has two kids back home in Vegas," Mark told him, staring at his computer screen.

"Really? So, a closet case by the sounds of things. Pays for sex with guys when he's away from home…or doesn't pay them, as was the case with Alex."

"So he hired Alex for sex, didn't pay him then called him and threatened to turn him in to the police for beating him up unless he paid him ten grand. The guy was seriously unhinged." Mark tapped a few keys on his keyboard. "You won't like this. Your friend Alex also has a record. He was arrested a year ago for solicitation of a police officer…"

"Ouch."

Mark sighed. "Yeah, but no jail time, just a heavy fine. Also arrested for domestic violence six months ago."

"What?"

"He beat up his boyfriend, David Summers, twenty-nine, who refused to press charges." Mark raised an eyebrow. "So beating up a client isn't such a stretch, maybe? No wonder he ran when you called me. But he knows you and I are married, right? Why involve you in this if he didn't want to deal with the police?"

"All good questions to which I have no answers." John echoed Mark's sigh. "Well, it's kinda out of my hands now…" He fished his cell out of his pocket as it buzzed. "Hey, Alex."

"Hey, man…" Alex sounded nervous. "I'm sorry I took off like that, but I freaked when you said you were calling the cops. I have a couple of things on my record that they're not gonna like."

"I know. Mark's just run a background on you. The domestic violence is going to look bad when the police question you."

Alex gasped. "Question me? But I didn't have anything to do with the guy's murder."

"Maybe not, but you were at the scene, you knew the guy—his name is Donald Forsythe, by the way—and you ran. There were two witnesses to that who gave the cops statements. I'm afraid it's now totally a police matter. I suggest you come in and not wait for them to issue a warrant for your arrest."

"I thought you were going to help me!"

"I will, any way I can, but it'll go a long way to you helping yourself if you come in willingly. Mark's here. D'you wanna talk to him?"

Alex sighed loudly. "What kind of choice do I have? Okay, let me talk to him."

John passed his phone over to Mark. "Hey, Alex. All I can do is repeat what John just told you. It'll be better for you if you come on in and talk to me."

"Are you going to arrest me?"

"Not if I think you're telling the truth."

"I didn't kill him, Mark. He was on the ground when I got there."

"Did you see anyone else…running away, maybe?"

"No…well, you know how the trees at the front of the park kind of obscure the view when you first get there? I thought I saw two men talking to who I presumed was the guy blackmailing me. I held back some in case he had brought backup. John said there was a chance he might bring some kind of heavies with him. When I went into the park, there was only him lying there…"

"Okay, that's why you need to come in and make an official statement. Do it, Alex, it'll benefit you in the end."

There was a long pause before Alex said, "Can I come tomorrow? I'm kinda shook up right now... nervous, you know?"

"Fine, be here at ten. I'll take your statement then. And, Alex...don't be a no-show, because that would mean I'd have to issue a warrant for your arrest. Okay?"

"Okay. I'll be there." He disconnected the call.

Mark gave John a long look. "What d'you think?"

"Hard to know. I didn't see Alex as the violent type, but beating up his boyfriend? Of course, we don't know the whole story...and punching someone is a long way from killing."

"Right, but it does show a vicious side to the man. Anyway, we'll get some news from Stan tomorrow after he's completed the autopsy, and we can maybe get some prints off the knife." He stretched his arms above his head and grinned at John. "Hungry? I could go for a pizza round about now."

"You buyin'?"

Mark snorted. "Hey, you're not a starving movie extra anymore. You could offer to go Dutch."

After a quick look into the bullpen to make sure no one was watching, John bent and gave Mark a long, slow kiss. "How about if I offer my body instead?" he murmured.

"There's a camera in here, you know," Mark mumbled against John's lips.

"Someone'll have fun checking the playback." He straightened and held out his hand to pull Mark from his chair. Their bodies connected and, as always, the flare of desire burned in John's blood. "We better get outta here before the camera picks up something really hot."

"Pizza to go, then?" Mark asked, his blue eyes darkening.

"You got it."

* * * *

John gazed up at his husband's sensuous expression, and not for the first or even the five hundredth time thought he was the luckiest man in the world, to be loved by someone as gorgeous as Mark. And it wasn't just those beautiful eyes and luscious mouth, nor the smooth skin over hard muscle, that made him such a prize. John loved him for the innate goodness in the man, the gift to see the best in people despite having been faced with some of the worst of humanity during his years in the police force. He'd seen that for himself a decade ago when they'd first met, when John had sat opposite Mark in an interrogation room expecting any minute to be slung behind bars and the key thrown away.

All these years later, and the love and admiration he had for Mark had never wavered. Even when his Italian stallion showed his stubborn streak.

"I love you," he whispered before encircling Mark's neck with his arms and bringing him down for a long, lingering kiss. He took Mark's muffled, humming response to mean *I love you too* and deepened their kiss, sliding his tongue over Mark's, loving the carnal heat that the meeting of their mouths generated. He arched into the pressure of Mark's body on top of him, grinding their erections together, hooking his legs around Mark's waist, holding Mark's body anchored to him.

After some more long and sensuous kisses, Mark eased John onto his stomach and ran his tongue down the length of John's spine to the cleft between his butt cheeks. John groaned with pleasure and writhed under Mark as he teased John's puckered opening with the tip of his tongue. Mark palmed each cheek, parting them to give himself greater access, then pushed in, dragging his tongue and lips around John's hole. John moaned and whimpered his ecstasy as Mark added a finger, using his saliva as lubricant, reaching in to stroke the sensitive gland inside John's tight passage. John raised his hips and wriggled his ass to take all of Mark's finger inside himself.

"Fuck me," he murmured. "Need you all the way inside me. Give me every one of those eight inches you know how to use so well." He turned onto his back and grinned up at Mark salaciously. "C'mon, give it to me as only you can."

Mark returned his sly grin with one that was pure sex. "Patience, my pretty." He reached for the lube.

"I put patience aside after the first time you fucked me." John ran his hands up and down the sides of Mark's muscular torso. He lifted his hips to meet Mark's slick fingers, drawing them in, writhing over them.

"God, but you are so fuckin' beautiful," Mark murmured, guiding his rock-hard cock between John's thighs. He pushed slowly forward and John moaned when Mark eased the broad head of his shaft into him. He raised himself and wrapped his arms around Mark's torso, holding him steady while he seated himself onto Mark's lap. With one quick, downward plunge, he took all of Mark's hot, throbbing dick inside him and moaned again with unadulterated satisfaction.

"Ungh…feels so good, Mark."

"Feels fantastic." Mark bucked his hips, driving himself deeper into John's tight heat, and John sank farther down on Mark's lap to take him all the way in. Wrapped in each other's arms, they moved to a slow and sensuous rhythm that wrenched moans of ecstasy from them both. John fell back onto the mattress, pulling Mark with him, and took his lips with a kiss that was an almost feverish union of lips, teeth and tongues. John was in heaven as Mark drove into him with powerful thrusts of his pelvis, the friction of flesh on flesh dizzying in its intensity. He gazed at his husband's face, caught in the rapture of near-orgasm, and his heart leapt when Mark gripped his erection, pumping the hard length with long, urgent strokes.

"So close," Mark muttered.

"Right there with you…" John arched himself into the solid heat of Mark's hard, muscled chest and cried out, holding Mark's heaving body tight against his own while they climaxed together. John's every nerve ending was on fire. His orgasm rolled over him and the hot surge of Mark's cum as he exploded inside him added to the exquisite pleasure that threatened to melt his brain. Mark collapsed over John and tightened his arms around him. He nuzzled the hollow under John's throat and kissed his sweat-slicked skin.

"Oh, my God," he whispered after a few moments had passed.

"*Thečhíȟila, ma-hiŋgnáku…*" John turned his head to murmur in Mark's ear.

Mark's chuckle sounded as if it came from deep inside his chest. "Love it when you talk dirty to me."

John poked him in the ribs. "You know what that means," he huffed.

"I do…" He kissed John's nose and smiled. "And I love you too, my husband."

Chapter Six

Mark called John at ten thirty. "Your friend Alex is a no-show," he said sounding totally pissed off. "I tried calling him, but I'm betting he didn't answer when he saw my name on his phone. I'll have to issue a warrant for the idiot's arrest, I'm afraid."

John groaned. "Idiot is right. Let me see if I can get hold of him."

"You can try, but if he doesn't get his butt in here within the next half-hour, I'll have no choice. If you talk to him, let him know that, and that he better get himself an attorney."

"Will do." John sighed. "I'll call you back."

"Fine, bye."

"Damn," John muttered under his breath as he punched in Alex's number. "Where the hell are you?" he snapped when Alex picked up. "And why didn't you answer Mark's call?"

"Me and David are on our way to Santa Barbara."

"What?" John couldn't believe what the man was telling him. "Are you crazy? You're supposed to be giving Mark your statement. He's gonna issue a warrant for your arrest if you don't show."

"Huh, they'll have to find me first."

"Alex! You think that's so difficult? You just made it ten times harder for yourself. And why are you dragging someone else into your mess?"

"David's my boyfriend and wanted to come with me."

John refrained from asking, *'Oh, the boyfriend you beat up six months ago?'* What was the point? The guy had made his decision to go with Alex and hopefully knew the consequences of running from the law. *Dumbasses.*

"Okay, if you turn around now and get to Mark's office within the next hour, you can still avoid arrest. But if you don't, just so long as you know, I can't help you any further."

"You were no fucking help anyway," Alex snarled. "I shoulda known better than to ask for help from someone who sucks a cop's dick. We're not gonna talk to *Mark* or any other cop. He'll just find an excuse to lock me up."

"Okay." John tamped down the anger that had heated his blood, before replying, "I guess we're done here, Alex. Good luck on the run. You'll need it." He cut the call before Alex could say anything else that might make their next meeting very awkward. He called Mark. "He's on the road heading for Santa Barbara."

"That stupid—! You know what kind of car he drives?"

"There was a red Chevy Malibu near where I parked the Harley. It was the only vehicle there, so I'm guessing that was his."

"Okay, I'll get an APB out."

"Oh, and by the way, he has the boyfriend with him."

"Terrific. I'll be in touch. Ciao."

"Ciao." He smiled at Millie as she brought him his mug filled with fresh coffee. "Thanks, Millie."

"You look like you need it more than usual," she remarked, frowning.

"Alex Vasquez, the guy who was in here yesterday?"

Millie nodded. "Tall, dark and brooding."

"The same. The guy he claimed was blackmailing him was stabbed to death in Jericho Park last night, and Alex fled the scene. Now he's on the run instead of meeting with Mark to clear himself of any involvement."

Millie tsked. "Not very bright."

"And he's got a record, Millie. Something he forgot to mention when he was here yesterday."

"Hmm... Good looks don't always reflect the character of the man, I'm afraid."

"Very profound, Millie," John said, grinning at her. "My grandmother would have agreed with you."

"A very wise woman, indeed." Millie sniffed and returned to her desk.

John sipped his coffee and mulled over the events of the past few days. He had to leave Alex to his fate, it seemed. There wasn't anything he could do for him now that he'd decided to try to beat the odds of being tracked down and arrested. His office phone rang, then Millie was on the intercom telling him that a Mr. Watkins was returning his call.

Watkins? Oh, yeah...the guy who wrote the article on civilian peacekeeping. He picked up. "Hi, Mr. Watkins. Thanks for returning my call. Are you back from your camping trip?"

"Actually, no, but it's not every day I get a call from a private detective with the intriguing name of John White Eagle. Is that your real name?"

"Yes, sir. My family is Dakota Sioux."

"Fascinating. So how can I help you?"

"I am investigating the disappearance of Samuel Andrews. Are you familiar with that name?"

"Why, yes, I've known Sam for several years. Disappearance, you say?"

"His sister, Penny, has hired me to find him. She hasn't heard from him in over a week, and according to her, that has never happened before. They're very close, she told me."

"Mmm, perhaps she thinks so." Watkins paused for a moment before adding, "I'm afraid young Penny has an overexaggerated opinion of their relationship. Sam was often quite irritated by her dependence on him."

"He told you this?" *Why am I not surprised to hear this?*

"Not in so many words, but we were on a mission in Afghanistan a few years ago and she proved herself to be…how can I say it without being rude?…a bit of a pest, I'm afraid. Constantly calling while we were in meetings or in the field. He started checking all his calls and not answering hers after a while. His expression, when he saw it was Penny calling, was one of exasperation, to say the least."

Well, this is interesting… "Did anything else happen in Afghanistan while you and Sam were there?"

"Yes, as a matter of fact. We got involved in a young Afghani man's kidnapping. Sam told us we had to save him, which we did. At the time, I didn't know how or why Sam knew the young man, but it was obvious there was a connection of some kind. Sam only said they'd met at one of the diplomatic cocktail parties we were invited to. One that I hadn't attended, obviously, or I would've remembered their meeting. Sam put himself in considerable danger during the operation, taking risks that at first I couldn't understand why he would."

He paused again before continuing. "The young man, when we found him with the help of one of his friends, had been badly beaten. Looked as if he'd been tortured, really. Sam was furious. He wanted to bring him back to the States for proper medical care. It wasn't possible, sadly—just too much red tape involved—but I know that Sam sent money for his hospital bills even when we got back home."

"So he kept in touch with this person?" John asked, his interest increasing as he listened to Watkins' information.

"As far as I know, yes. Not surprising really. Just between you and me, I think Sam was more than just fond of Jareem. That was the young man's name."

John smiled. So Ellis Watkins was a bit of a gossip...and gossips could be very useful. And again, if Sam was gay, that blew Penny's story about how close she and her brother were. She had been quick to assure him that Sam was not gay when John had asked.

"Do you know what happened to...uh, Jareem?"

"Well..." Watkins paused yet again. "I don't know if I should give away Sam's secrets so easily. He might be annoyed with me for giving you as much information as I have."

"Believe me, Mr. Watkins," John said gently, "anything you can tell me will make it easier for me to find Sam Andrews. It sounds like he might be in some kind of trouble, and I'd really like to help him out if I can."

"Right..." Watkins inhaled sharply. "You're a private detective, after all. That's what you do, right? I do know that Sam has been back to Afghanistan to visit Jareem more than once. It's not an easy country to obtain a visa for, yet Sam has managed to arrange it, so I think I'm right when I say that there is more than just friendship between Sam and Jareem. I believe Sam has very strong feelings for Jareem."

"So..." John couldn't help but think that Watkins had turned out to be his best source of information. "Now that I've told you that Sam Andrews has disappeared, what's your best guess as to where he might be?"

"Honestly, I don't know," Watkins said. "I haven't spoken with him in over a month, but the last time we did speak, he certainly didn't intimate that he was thinking of going AWOL, or anything like that. I am surprised by this news."

"Would he have gone back to Afghanistan if Jareem had asked him to, or if he heard from some source or another that Jareem was in difficulties?"

"Yes, to both of those options, without a doubt."

Really. Don't think Penny Andrews is gonna pony up for my fare to Afghanistan. "Well, thank you, Mr. Watkins, you've been very helpful. Oh, by the way, I spoke with Mr. Andrews Senior, and he told me he'd heard from his son three, or maybe four, days ago now."

"Unlikely. There definitely was no love lost between father and son. I met Andrews Senior only once, but it was enough to convince me the man was the bully Sam accused him of being. In business and in his personal life, according to Sam."

"Well, if you should hear from him, please tell him to call his sister and put her mind at ease."

"Oh, of course. Although, knowing Sam, I really don't think she should worry too much. Wherever Sam is, he'll be in control of the situation. That's just the way he is."

John sat back in his chair after he'd disconnected the call and tried to put together everything that had been said about Sam Andrews, conflicting opinions though they might be. From what he'd read about Sam Andrews, Ellis Watkins' view of him seemed closer to the mark. The man was handsome, an adventurer, obviously willing to take risks if the account Watkins had given of Andrews pursuing Jareem's kidnappers was factual. And just like Andrews' friend Richards, Watkins had expressed the opinion that his sister shouldn't worry about him too much because Sam Andrews could handle himself well enough to survive. He hoped they were both correct in that assumption.

He drummed his fingers alongside his phone before picking it up and calling Penny Andrews. "Hi, Miss Andrews, I have couple of questions for you. You have a minute?"

"Of course. Have you found out anything?"

John chuckled. "I'm the one with the questions, remember?"

"Oh, yes."

"Just kidding. Anyway, I spoke with Ellis Watkins today. Does that name ring a bell?"

"Um...vaguely."

"He says he's known your brother for several years and had gone on a peacekeeping mission with him in Afghanistan. Does that make him less vague?"

"Uh, yes, but I've never actually met him."

"I see. Does the name Jareem mean anything to you?"

There was such a long silence that John had to check his phone to see if she had hung up on him. "Yes," she said finally, her voice low and flat.

"Is there a possibility that your brother has gone to Afghanistan to see Jareem?"

"Why on earth would he do that?" Now her voice held a sharp tone.

"Let me level with you, Miss Andrews. I've gotten a lot of conflicting reports from the people I've spoken to since I took on your case, so I threw it all in a hat, shook it up a little and came to this conclusion. Your brother is either gay or bisexual, and probably in love with the man named Jareem he rescued from a kidnapping some years ago. According to Mr. Watkins, Jareem had been tortured and your bro wanted to bring him back to the States for proper medical treatment, but that wasn't possible, so he paid the hospital bills, and has been back to visit Jareem more than once. Were you aware of these situations when you came to see me the other day?"

Again, Penny Andrews withdrew into silence, so John continued. "If I had to guess as to where your brother is now, it would be Afghanistan."

"I was praying you wouldn't say that," she said dully.

"So you did have an inkling that it was possible?"

"I tried to talk him out of it," she blurted. "The last big fight Sam and my father had was all about this…this *fixation* he has about going back to Afghanistan to get Jareem out. Jareem is a lost cause, John. He's been targeted by a religious sect because he's gay, and even by his own family. He's been in hiding for over a year and now—if you're right, and I hate to admit that you probably are—Sam has gone back to help him...*again*."

"And you're against him trying to help the guy...you and your father, both, by the sounds of it. This would be the stupidity your father said Sam might be mixed up in. Am I right?"

"Yes, and it's not only stupid. It puts Sam in terrible danger. You have no idea what it's like out there. Nor did I until Sam went on that mission and told me how awful it was. People are murdered every day and no one ever brought to justice for it. ISIS, the Taliban, just for a start. Young boys and girls are kidnapped all the time and sold into slavery. Despite the US military presence there, it's one of the most dangerous places in the world. Even Kabul, the capital, is a dangerous place."

"How did Sam meet Jareem? I'm presuming he confided in you, as you were so close." John kept the sarcasm out of his voice, even though he knew now that Penny was exaggerating the closeness of their bond.

"Yes, he told me. He was at some diplomatic function, and Jareem was there with his father. I don't know how Jareem and Sam got talking. Some signal between them that gay men have, I suppose."

John rolled his eyes but said nothing in response. It was possible that Jareem had been a hook-up, but things had obviously escalated since then. Three years was a long time to still be enthralled by a casual pickup.

"So, it begs the question, why ask me to find him when you had a pretty good idea where he was?"

She sighed. "Because I was hoping against hope that even though he'd disappeared, he hadn't gone back there, that you'd find something that would lead you to find him in the States. It was worth a try, anyway. I hadn't reckoned on you talking to that nosy Ellis Watkins. Sam spent far too much time in that old geezer's company."

Nice. John frowned. "Well, now that we have a good idea where he is, I guess you'll just have to wait for him to come home, with or without Jareem."

She gasped. "Oh, God. Our father will have a fit if he brings him here. But I can't for the life of me see how he possibly can. It would take a miracle to spirit Jareem out of Kabul. There's no way he can come out of hiding. He'd be picked up immediately and imprisoned…and Sam along with him, if they even bother with that."

John heard the sob that sounded as if it were wrenched from her. He felt bad. Penny Andrews had gone down in his estimation from the frail but likeable young lady he'd met two days ago. But it was obvious she cared about her brother, despite her readiness to lie about his sexual orientation. No doubt his imprisonment or demise in a foreign country would be hard on her.

"I'm sorry I can't do more for you, Miss Andrews," he said with sympathy. "Perhaps things will turn out okay."

"Perhaps. Well, thank you. Send me your bill for the rest of your time."

"That's okay. It's paid in full."

"Oh, okay then. Goodbye, Mr. White Eagle."

"Bye, and good luck."

John put his phone down and was struck by the strangest feeling that he might not have heard the last of the Andrews family.

* * * *

Mark was already home when John got to their house. "This is a nice surprise," he said after a long hug and kiss from Mark.

"Best part of my day, every day, is coming home to you," Mark told him, nuzzling his ear.

"You say all the right things to make me want to drag you into bed."

Mark chuckled. "Have I mentioned that you're easy?"

"And flexible, don't forget."

Mark kissed him again. "How could I forget that? Anyway..." He stepped back and went into the kitchen. "Like a beer?"

John followed him. "Yeah, sounds good. How was your day?"

"You go first. Give me the latest on your missing person case." He popped the tab on a beer can then handed it to John.

"It could be that Sam isn't missing after all," John said. "He might, however, be in some trouble. Sounds like he went off to Afghanistan in search of the man he loves."

Mark gave him a raised-eyebrow stare. "Wow, that's a shift in the story."

"It sure is, and it's what both Penny Andrews and her father suspected. She was just hoping against hope, I guess, that it wasn't so. That I would find out he was, as you suggested, taking a sabbatical or out on a dig somewhere. Anyway, nothing more I can do. He'll come back eventually, I imagine, with or without his boyfriend...or not."

They both took long swigs of their beer, then Mark said, "So, Alex. He and his boyfriend were seen at a gas station the other side of Carpinteria. The mini-market attendant recognized Alex from the online photos we circulated. He called the local cops, but by the time they got there, of course Alex was long gone. The kid did get the license plate, and you were right, it's a red Chevy he's driving. We've got an alert going on Interstate Five, so it won't be long before he's brought in."

John sighed. "I just don't get why he ran like that." He clinked his beer can against Mark's then took a long swallow of the cold brew.

"Well, I did a background check on his boyfriend, David Summers, and guess what? He has a record too. Bit more serious than Alex's. He did time for peddling drugs and receiving stolen goods. I'm thinking the reason they ran is he's still on the game."

"Shit. Why in hell did Alex get himself mixed up with a frickin' criminal? Maybe that's what their fight was about…and how do we know this David guy didn't force Alex into running?"

Mark sipped his beer. "Did he sound as if he was being forced when you spoke to him last?"

"No, he was more angry with me than anything."

"Well, we'll have to wait till they're found and questioned for the answers we need." Mark stared at John expectantly. "So, what are you making for dinner?"

John chuckled. "Nothing you'd want to eat." John's skills did not include cooking, but as he'd told Mark many times, he had other ways of keeping him happy.

"Just as well I stopped at the deli on the way home," Mark said. "I picked up a to-go lasagna and salad. The lasagna's in the oven."

"Thought I could smell something really good—apart from you, that is." He leaned in to sniff at Mark's neck. "Mmm, sexy man."

"I didn't get dessert," Mark told him. "Figured you'd do."

John smirked and put his arms around Mark's waist. "So, let's have me for dessert first, lasagna second. Okay?"

"That's my boy."

Chapter Seven

The following day, Alex and his boyfriend had still not been apprehended, and John sympathized with Mark's frustration, as he told Millie while they shared a coffee in his office.

"Is this Alex a very good friend of yours?" Millie asked.

"Not really." John thought back on how he'd met Alex. "We worked together and hung out a few times, but usually with some of the other guys either in the film crew or the cast. We were never *buddy* buddies, if you know what I mean. I hadn't seen him in years before he came here to talk the other day. However, his actions have been a bit surprising. Mark told me that the boyfriend did time for drug pushing, so it makes me wonder if Alex is as innocent as he said he is."

"You mean about the murder?" Millie peered at him over the rim of her coffee mug.

"Like I said, I don't know Alex all that well, but I can't see him as a killer. However, the boyfriend, David Summers, might have been in touch with guys from his prison time who have fewer scruples. Alex said he saw two men in the park maybe talking with Donald Forsythe, the guy that ended up dead. One of them could have been David Summers? Alex may not have known his boyfriend was going to off Forsythe, but he had to know once he got home. Even if Summers had hired a couple of guys to do the deed. So it begs the question, was that why they both took off together?"

"Or did Alex's boyfriend tell him their only option was to run?" Millie mused. "Alex might even have been going to turn the boyfriend in."

John nodded. "Very possible…" John's cell rang at that moment. "Might be Mark." He frowned on seeing the name of the caller and pressed the Speaker button. "Hi, Miss Andrews. What can I do for you?"

"It's about Sam." It was obvious she was crying, hiccupping through her sobs.

Oh, shit… Has his body been found?

He breathed a sigh of relief when Penny said, "He called me about an hour ago to tell me he and Jareem were on the run. Then he asked if I could get Dad to call his friend Senator Davies to help them. He'd approached the ambassador's office in Kabul, but the staff were up to their eyes with problems following a car bomb incident in a busy part of town. There was no one available to give him any kind of aid. Dad refused, just as I knew he would, and he was very rude about it."

John's hackles rose when Penny continued. "He told me to let Sam know he could never bring 'that boy' into his home. He was vile, actually. Made me wonder if he was becoming unhinged, the things he said. I hung up on him and called Dave Richards, but he was absolutely no help. Said he couldn't possibly get involved in anything as crazy as that. I don't know what to do, Mr. White Eagle."

"Call me John."

"What? Oh yes. I want to help Sam, but I'm at a loss as to how to do it." She was crying again. "Can you help me, John? I know your husband is a policeman. He might have some contacts who could intervene on Sam's behalf."

John glanced at Millie, who had been busy scribbling on the pad she carried everywhere with her. She slipped a note in front of John, who read it quickly.

Tell her you'll call her back in a few minutes.

"Uh, let me check on that for you, Miss Andrews, and I'll call you back in a few minutes."

"Oh, all right."

"In just a few minutes, I promise," John said on hearing the doubt in her voice. He hung up and gazed at Millie expectantly.

"Did I mention that my late husband was in the diplomatic service for many years?"

"No, I don't think you did," John told her. "I thought he worked in a bookshop."

"That came after he retired. For years, he was a member of the diplomatic service and we visited several countries during that time." She smiled at John's slightly awed expression. "You probably don't see me in an evening gown, attending glittering functions in Paris and London, but I even met the Queen on one occasion and Putin on another. Nasty man with a very sneaky leer, but he knew how to wine and dine in style."

"Wow," John murmured. "You are a surprise a day, Millie. So, you know someone who might be able to help Penny Andrews' brother?"

"If the one I'm thinking of is still active…or even if not, there may be others who could help. It's certainly worth a try."

"It sure is. How long d'you think it'll take to get in touch with him?"

"*Her,* actually. Audrey Melville. She and her husband Arthur Melville were both in the service. Arthur died a few years ago, and it's been a few months since Audrey and I talked, but I should manage to get hold of her quite quickly. I'll try right now."

John smiled as he watched Millie stride over to her desk like a woman on a mission. Which she was. If she could pull off getting Sam Andrews out of the trouble he was obviously in, then kudos to Millie, and he'd make darned sure there'd be big thanks from the Andrews family…or at least from Penny. He listened to Millie's laughter as she no doubt caught up with her friend's news of the past months.

In the meantime, he did some double-checking on Alex's boyfriend, David Summers. He was twenty-nine and, from his mug shot, not bad-looking, though he'd definitely been on some kind of drugs when the photograph had been taken—five years ago, according to the report. His eyes were unfocused, his hair was all over the place and the T-shirt he was wearing was ripped at the shoulder.

Where in hell did Alex meet this character? Now, as he stared at Summers' photo, he could well believe that the guy might have organized Donald Forsythe's murder. Although why he'd do it when he knew Alex would be at the scene was something John couldn't fathom. Or had Alex been in on the murder? He hated to think it was so, but Alex running then leaving town put him in a bad position.

He looked up as Millie entered his office, a bright smile on her face. "Audrey said she'll make some calls to people she knows who understand the situation in Afghanistan. It may take some time, of course, so perhaps you should call Miss Andrews and try to put her mind at ease...at least let her know that you're attempting to help."

"Thanks, Millie." He grinned at her. "You've been with me for almost a year and I'm still learning things about you. You'll be telling me you were a secret agent next."

"Not quite. Just let's say, I've been around."

Chuckling, John picked up his phone and punched in Penny Andrews' number. "Hi, again. Looks like we might have some help for your brother."

"Oh, that's wonderful."

Yeah, if we can pull it off. "I can't tell you much more than that right now," he added. "As you can imagine, it might take some time before we hear anything. So just hold tight."

"I will, and thank you, John."

"Welcome. Talk to you soon."

* * * *

A week went by without any word from Millie's friend, Audrey Melville, and John was frankly worried that it was a no-go, although Millie still seemed optimistic. In the meantime, Alex and David Summers had been apprehended by the Santa Barbara police after a tip-off from a motel clerk.

"Apparently," Mark told John later when he called, "Summers had pissed the guy off over towels not being changed in the room. He ranted at the desk clerk for so long that it gave the guy a lot of time for Summers' face to register as someone the police were searching for. He called nine-one-one soon as Summers left in a huff despite getting his clean towels. So, the lesson to be learned here is, never piss off a motel clerk when you're on the run."

"Where are they now?" John asked, chuckling at Mark's twisted sense of humor.

"Being held overnight by the Santa Barbara police. They'll be transported to LA to be summarily charged with trying to avoid arrest in connection with an ongoing murder investigation."

John sighed. "I can't help but feel sorry for Alex. I think he got himself way in over his head with Summers. He was great to be around when we worked together."

"But he's an adult, John. Free to make his own choices. He's just making the wrong ones, that's all."

"I guess, still..."

"Any word on the Sam Andrews situation?"

"Nope. Nice way to change the subject," John said wryly. "From one tetchy case to another."

Mark chuckled. "Don't forget we're going over to Dad's for dinner tonight."

"No way I'd forget that. He puts both of us to shame in the cooking stakes."

"True, that. Anyway, I'll see you over there at six thirty. I have a couple of things to take care of before I can leave."

"That means I'll have my bike and you'll have your car."

Mark snickered. "You're quick, but what's your point?"

"Well, I won't get to ride home with you...play with your dick...suck you off while you drive. That's my point, husband mine."

"Jesus, John...not while I'm at work...and can't Millie hear you?"

"She left, so I can say all kinds of dirty things to you. Get you nice and hard so you can't stand up—"

"I'm going now!"

Laughing, John disconnected the call.

* * * *

John loved going to his father-in-law's house. Never having known his own father, John had taken to Jack's warm and caring personality right away. He'd told Mark time and again that he was a lucky so-and-so to have such a great dad. Mark's mom had died a year earlier and John had secretly wished that he could introduce Jack to his mother, but she lived in South Dakota and wouldn't dream of living in a city like Los Angeles.

"So much traffic," she'd complained the one time she'd visited John and Mark to see their new house. *"So much chaos everywhere."* She'd gone around their house muttering under her breath.

"Is she angry?" Mark had asked.

"No, she's saying spirit prayers for us to be safe here, for our home to be a haven of peace and tranquility."

"That's nice..."

When John had met Mark, he'd been a hair's-breadth away from being locked up as a murder suspect. Having met Mark's dad under those conditions had made John nervous, but the older man had shown his non-judgmental character even then.

"Any friend of Mark's is a friend to me, too. If he says you're innocent, I believe it." After John and Mark had gotten married, he'd asked Jack if he could call him Dad. He'd been thrilled when Jack had hugged him and said, *"Only if I can call you son."*

Jack was out front of his house raking leaves when John pulled up on his Harley. Jack threw down the rake and beamed at John as he jumped off his bike and ran to meet him. A back-slapping hug ensued.

"How was your night out with the guys?" John asked.

"Great," Jack replied putting his arm around John's shoulders and leading him into the house. "So many tall stories, as usual, but they're a good bunch on the whole. Mark called and said he'd be late. We can enjoy a beer together till he gets here. You okay on that bike with one drink?"

John chuckled. "Long as you feed me too." He followed Jack through the house to the kitchen, where Jack fished two cans of Bud from the fridge and handed one to John. "Here's lookin' at ya." Jack smacked his can against John's. "How's that missing person case you took on going?"

"It's complicated." John related what Penny Andrews had told him. "Millie, my secretary—"

"A fine woman, that Millie," Jack interrupted. "You're a lucky man to have such an intelligent and attractive lady working for you."

"Yes, I am," John replied, somewhat surprised by Jack's statement.

"Tell her I said hello when you see her tomorrow."

"Uh, yes, I will." *Does he have a thing for Millie?* He'd have to run that by Mark, see what he thought. He cleared his throat. "Anyway, she called some lady she was in the diplomatic service with to see if she knew anyone who could help. So that's where we are at the moment. I'm just hoping Andrews can keep out of sight until we can get him help."

"What about the embassy?"

"They weren't too helpful before, but maybe Millie's friend can find the right person to get them help. Andrews' friend might have to ask for asylum, and from what I've learned about that process, it can take a long time. I don't know if they'll want Andrews hanging around…or even if he can afford to. He has some lecture dates lined up in Orange County next month that he'll have to cancel if he can't get back in time."

"Complicated for sure, as you said. And the friend you were in movies with…Alex, was it? What about him?"

John sighed. "That's a mess. Alex has got himself mixed up with an unsavory character he says is his boyfriend. Anyway, they're refusing to cooperate with the police so they're being held pending charges while they wait for the boyfriend's attorney to show up. Mark's working on that one…probably why he said he'd be late."

"Hey, guys…"

"Speak of the devil." Jack turned at the sound of his son's voice. "Thought you were going to be late."

Mark hugged his dad. "Had to let Alex and his boyfriend go. Summers got himself a good attorney." Mark snorted. "He made it sound like they were on a road trip, didn't know they were needed for questioning."

"What a crock," John said, accepting Mark's kiss on his cheek and pat on his butt.

"It's far from over." Mark told them. "We just have to find some evidence that at least Summers is connected to Forsythe's murder, which, now I've spoken to the guy, I'm more than convinced he is. He is a total nutjob. How Alex let himself get pulled into a relationship with him is beyond me."

"How was Alex?" John asked.

"Subdued the whole time. Said practically nothing."

"Sounds like he's under the boyfriend's control," Jack remarked, handing Mark a beer.

"Doesn't sound like the Alex I know…or knew, rather," John said after chugging the last of his beer from the can. "He was always the macho man. 'Course, I haven't met the boyfriend."

"Trust me, you don't want to." Mark took John's arm and they followed Jack out to the patio, where he already had the grill fired up. "The guy's psycho. Flies off the handle at the drop of a hat. Screamed at me when I tried to have him answer the simplest question, like why did you take off? I expected him to start foaming at the mouth any second. What a headcase. Alex just sat there. When the attorney arrived, Summers calmed down a bit. It was obvious they knew each other well, and Summers let him take charge. We had to release them because we had nothing to back up the possible charge. Summers knew that. He was gloating when the attorney laid it out…charge them or release them."

They sat at the patio table, watching Jack at the grill flipping the steaks and adding some of his 'secret' ingredients. John nudged Mark with his elbow.

"You have to get him to tell you what that is…or steal the jar, or something."

Mark laughed. "No way will he ever give that up."

"Maybe I'll put the recipe in my will," Jack said, turning to smirk at John, who groaned.

"No fair, Dad," he whined. "You'll live to be a hundred and I still won't be able to grill a steak that'll satisfy Mark the way yours do."

Jack chuckled. "Well, you'll just have to keep on satisfying him the best way you can."

Mark burst out laughing and John pretended to be scandalized. "Don't know what you mean," he huffed.

"Well, if you don't know by now, can't think why Mark's always got that shit-eatin' grin on his face when he's around you."

John really did love his father-in-law.

* * * *

Three days later, the insistent chiming of his cell phone woke John from a hot dream of Mark rimming him. He tried to ignore the annoying noise and hold on to the dream, but it was no use. The vision and sensations faded into nothingness. Muttering under his breath, he picked up his cell and squinted at the screen.

Four a.m. and I don't know this number. "Uh…John White Eagle here. Who's this?" There was so much static on the line that John could barely make out the voice on the other end. "Say again."

"Sam Andrews…I want to thank you."

Thank me? "Where are you, Sam?"

"We're on a military plane on the way to Berlin."

We. "That's great news, but this is a shit-awful connection. Can you maybe call me when you get to Berlin?"

"Will do. Can't thank you enough." The line went dead.

"That sounded interesting," Mark mumbled, throwing an arm around John.

"Sam Andrews is on his way to Berlin. Millie's friend must've come through."

"Great." He tightened his arm around John and nuzzled his neck. "Go back to sleep. We'll talk about it in the morning."

"It's already morning, and I'm kinda buzzed from that news." He turned to face Mark. "Wanna fool around?"

"No."

"Yes, you do. I can *feel* you do."

Mark groaned. "You know how old I'm gonna be next birthday?"

"Yeah." John kissed him. "Forty years young, with the body of an athlete and…" He slid a hand the length of Mark's torso and stroked his cock. "The dick I love to suck."

Mark groaned again, but this time it sounded more like need. "You win," he murmured, kissing John's lips. "As always."

Chapter Eight

Millie was excited when John told her about Sam Andrews' call. "I knew Audrey would come through."

"Yeah, we have to get Andrews to meet her. He kept thanking me, but it's your friend he needs to thank…and you."

"Audrey won't expect it, but it wouldn't be a bad idea if they met," Millie said. "If he wants to keep galivanting off to foreign shores these days, he could use a reliable contact."

John nodded. "He's going to call from Berlin, so anytime now, I expect. He said *we*, by the way, which I guess includes Jareem. One thing for sure, Andrews Senior is not going to be happy about this. Penny told me he's never going to allow Sam to bring Jareem to his house. No big loss, in my opinion. Apparently, the last major row between father and son was about Sam wanting to bring Jareem to the States. So there's that for him to contend with."

"What a pity." Millie frowned. "Life's not hard enough? The father should be ashamed of himself for not supporting his son. He sounds horrible."

"Ellis Watkins called him a bully. I think that's a fair assumption." He glanced at his cell as it chimed. "I think this is him. Hello? John White Eagle here."

"Hi, John. Okay if I call you John? This is Sam Andrews."

"Of course you can." He pressed the Speaker button so Millie could hear. "You're in Berlin?"

"Yes. Jareem and myself. The embassy finally returned one of my hundred calls. They gave Jareem a temporary passport and a flight on a troop plane leaving that afternoon. Amazing what they can do when they want to."

"Or are shamed into it by members of the diplomatic service. Audrey Melville…"

"Ah, yes." Sam chuckled. "Her name was spoken with a mixture of annoyance and reverence. I have to meet her."

"You will, and her friend who just happens to be my secretary, Millie Barnum. When will you be stateside?"

"Probably in a couple of days. We're not out of the woods yet, I'm afraid. Jareem has enemies in Kabul who won't give up until they know he's been punished."

"Punished for what?"

"Being who he is…a gay man, and in love with me, a vile American. Which brings me to ask for another favor."

"Oh, yes?"

"Jareem…" Sam paused for a moment before continuing. "I'm guessing you understand the relationship between us?"

"Yes, although I have to tell you, your sister seemed to be in denial of the fact you're gay."

Sam sighed. "She and my father both. Neither one understands my feelings for Jareem, so for that reason I can't rely on them for help with our situation. Which brings me back to the favor-asking. Is there any possible way you could give us a room in your place for a couple of nights? You have an apartment or a house?"

"Uh, Mark, that's my husband...we recently bought a house in North Hollywood. Wait, you don't have a place in LA?"

"Yes, but I've already been warned it's most likely not safe. The extremist religious sect that targeted Jareem in Kabul has followers in California. It's not too much of a stretch to imagine they've been informed as to where I live." Sam paused to clear his throat, before continuing, "It'll only be for a couple of nights till I can find a place with security. I'd really appreciate the help."

"Gotcha. Okay, let me know what your schedule is, and I'll pick you up at the airport." He would have to clear the arrangement with Mark, but he didn't see a problem with him agreeing.

"Ah, that's really great. I'll call you when we can get a flight to LAX arranged. Thanks again, John. I look forward to meeting you. Bye for now."

"Yeah, good luck." He called Mark and apprised him of his conversation with Sam Andrews. "I said yes to him staying with us for a couple of nights. Hope that's okay."

"Yes, although they might be better off in a safe house. Bit hard to organize at such short notice, though, but if he can't find somewhere suitable with security, I'll talk to the chief."

John sat back in his chair after Mark had ended the call. "So, what d'you think, Millie?"

She frowned. "I'm not sure I like the idea of you giving them a room in your house. If there are, as he seems to think, people out to target this Jareem, you could be putting yourself and Mark in danger."

"Mark and me can take care of ourselves…and each other."

"Mark and I," Millie corrected him. "And that's as maybe, but why take the chance? Have Mark turn this over to the FBI. The people after Jareem sound like terrorists and should be investigated."

"You're right. I'll talk to Mark tonight. He did mention getting a safe house for them, so maybe that's a better idea."

Millie pursed her lips before saying, "A *much* better idea, John."

"I better let his sister know what's going on. I'm hoping she'll be happy with the news that her brother is coming home."

"But not alone," Millie remarked, dryly.

"Right, not alone. I'll let her know I'm picking them up at the airport. Somehow, I don't imagine there'll be a welcoming committee consisting of her and dear old Dad. Oh, by the way…" He thought he'd just throw this out, see what kind of reaction he got from Millie. "We had dinner with Mark's dad last night."

"How is the dear man?"

Dear man… She calls him dear man, and Jack thinks she's intelligent and attractive. Hmm… "He's good. Still fighting fit. He said to say hello."

"Well, you tell him the same when you see him next."

"I certainly will," Mark said, grinning.

* * * *

"There isn't a safe house available in LA," Mark told him when they connected later in the day. "The nearest is in San Diego, so we should probably take them to our place for the one or two nights they need, and if something becomes available, we can transfer them."

"And in the meantime, Sam might find a suitable apartment or house," John said. "Can't believe his father won't give them shelter."

"Well, we don't know what's really at the root of all that hostility between them."

"No, but it's bad enough for Penny Andrews to think the old man might have done away with Sam."

"*If* you can believe what she says," Mark pointed out. "From what you've told me, I'm not sure I can regard her opinions as totally sound. Oh, and the by way, Alex called me. He wants to come in and give a statement...without the boyfriend."

"Oh, yeah? Wonder what brought about this change of heart."

"He sounded tense, so I'm guessing he and Summers had a falling out. Anyway, we'll find out when he comes in. I'll keep you apprised."

"Thanks. I'm glad he's seen the sense of talking to you. I just hope he hasn't put himself in danger." John sighed. "Anyway, see you at home later. Love you."

"Yep. Bye. Love you too."

Millie was preparing to leave. "Millie, why don't you take tomorrow off? Have a long weekend. Looks like I'll be tied up with getting Sam and Jareem settled so we'll just have the calls, if any, go to voicemail and deal with them on Monday."

"If you're sure," Millie said. "But you can call me in case of any emergencies."

"I'll do that. Have a nice weekend."

"You too, John...and please take care. Mark too."

Later, John left the office and headed for the grocery store near their house. It was his turn to get dinner, a task he did not enjoy. One of these days, he or Mark had to join some kind of cooking class. Three times weekly at the gym wouldn't always combat eating pizza and takeout. He'd tried watching easy recipe videos on YouTube, but without success. What those chefs made look so *easy* ended up being something no one would want to put near their mouths by the time John was finished with it.

The local store had a rack of pre-cooked chickens that smelled delicious. That would do. *Even I can't screw up something that's already been cooked by experts.* He grabbed one and a bag of salad. As he stood in line to pay, his cell rang.

"John White Eagle."

"Hi, John. It's Sam. We're at the airport in Berlin. I managed to get us a red-eye flight out tonight."

"That's great. What time do you get to LAX?"

"We have to change planes in New York, so ETA with the time differential is one p.m. tomorrow. Hope that's okay."

"No problem. We can discuss arrangements when you get here. How're you guys holding up?"

"It's been nerve-wracking, to be honest." Sam's sigh was long and hard. "I just have to keep Jareem safe. But

I know we've done the right thing. Again, thank you, John."

"Like I said, no problem. Have a safe flight. See you tomorrow." John paid for his stuff and left the store. Millie's words rankled in his head. Maybe he shouldn't have been okay with inviting Sam and Jareem to stay with him and Mark. He had to admit to a certain uneasiness in having the men in their house, but it was done, and wouldn't it look mean to change his mind now? If only there had been a safe house to take them to… But what was the worst that could happen? He and Mark were totally capable of dealing with any off-the-wall religious sect that tried any funny business.

Years ago, when they'd first met, Mark had trained him in the kind of martial combat used by the police force, and even now, along with his tri-weekly workouts, he attended a martial arts class. His knowledge of defensive moves had come in handy on more than just a few occasions when faced with angry and overly aggressive people on the wrong side of the law.

John stowed the chicken and salad in his carrier box and set off for home, his mind filled with the expectation of meeting Sam Andrews. He had no doubt that the man was someone he was sure Mark and he would enjoy meeting. Too bad the circumstances weren't the best, but the chances of them connecting in any other way were remote, to say the least. The guy had balls for sure. Heading into dangerous territory to bring back the man he loved…it was movie material, in John's opinion. He just hoped things would work out for them once they were stateside.

Mark was home when John arrived, and not in a good mood. "Alex was a no-show again," he said bitterly before John could even get close enough for a kiss hello.

"What the fuck's the matter with him?" John burrowed into Mark's arms anyway and kissed his neck.

Mark sighed and returned John's kiss. "Who the hell knows? I sent officers to his place to bring him in. There was no sign of him or Summers, or their vehicles. Looks like they were stupid enough to make a run for it again. I issued an APB so they won't get far." He stepped back from John's embrace. "You smell like food."

John chuckled and held up the bag he was carrying. "Roast chicken…cooked by someone who knows what they're doing."

"Not you, obviously." Mark grinned at him.

"Hey!" John tried to look offended, but it was the truth, so he ended up laughing instead. "If you hadn't beaten me home, I would've put it in the oven and pretended it was all me. Yeah, like you'd have believed that."

Mark followed him into the kitchen. "You have many wonderful attributes, babe." He patted John's butt. "I'm staring at one now…but fixing a meal ain't in there."

"Sadly, you're right." John turned on the oven and put the chicken in. "I got salad too." He put the bag in the fridge and brought out two beers. "Sam called. They'll be at LAX at one p.m. I said I'd pick them up."

Mark nodded as he took the beer John handed him. "You'll be able to stay with them till I get home?"

"Yeah, I told Millie to take the day off. By the way, she's not happy with Sam and Jareem staying here, even if it's only for a couple of days."

"Can't say I am either, but probably for different reasons. The house is secure and it's unlikely the bad guys' intelligence is so good they'll know within a day or so where Sam is." Mark finished his beer. "Want another?"

"When we eat. You know what a lightweight I am when it comes to demon liquor."

"Okay, so tomorrow, I'm thinking the guys are gonna be exhausted by the time they get here. So we should just let them sleep. Talking can wait."

"They might be hungry."

"Yeah, well, we'll go out or order in. No way are we subjecting them to our brand of home-style cooking!"

* * * *

LAX was its usual expected chaos when John arrived at twelve forty-five. He'd checked Delta arrivals from New York online and Sam's flight was scheduled to land more or less on time. He scanned the large crowd waiting in the terminal but couldn't really pinpoint anyone who looked the least bit suspicious. *Silly to even try,* he thought. Any flight from New York would be filled with people from so many diverse races and cultures—a religious extremist would hardly stand out.

As passengers streamed into the baggage claim area, signs from waiting limo drivers were hoisted overhead. He was momentarily distracted when he spotted Sam and Jareem walking toward the bag carousel. Sam looked very much like his photograph, blond and handsome, although he was taller than John had expected. His gaze flicked back over to the signs and... *Shit.* One read *Samuel Andrews*. Had his sister hired a driver for him? Why would she when he'd told her he was going to pick her brother up? For sure it wouldn't be Andrews Senior.

"Sam! Over here." He walked in front of Sam and Jareem. "You expecting a limo?"

"No way." Sam's appraising glance ended up over John's shoulder and he grimaced. "Already?" he whispered.

John turned and quickly approached the sign holder, a small man with a thick mustache. He checked the guy's jacket for any telltale bulge that he might be armed. Seeing nothing, he said, "What a coincidence. I'm here to pick up Mr. Andrews too. What's your drop-off point?"

"What?" the man muttered.

"Where are you taking Mr. Andrews?"

"To his hotel."

"He's lying." Sam was at John's side, a hand on Jareem's arm.

"Which hotel?" John asked. The man turned to go, but John grabbed his jacket. "Who sent you?"

The man lobbed a punch at John's face, but John was quicker and the guy's fist missed by a mile. Around them, people gasped and backed away as John struggled with the would-be abductor. Showing a lot of strength for a little guy, he wrenched himself free of John's grasp and sprinted away toward the exit. John was about to give chase, but Sam stopped him.

"Just get us out of here, before someone alerts Security," he rasped. "They didn't waste any time trying to get to us."

"You have bags?"

"Just what we're carrying."

"Let's go then."

They hurried toward the exit. John didn't think it sensible pausing for introductions when it was obvious that they were being monitored by unfriendly forces even here in LAX. Once they reached his rental car and got them inside, he held out his hand.

"Glad you made it here safely."

Sam smiled, the corners of his ice-blue eyes crinkling as he took John's hand in his. "Thanks to you, and your awareness back there that something was wrong." He turned slightly in his seat. "This is Jareem. Jareem, this is the man I have told you about. John White Eagle."

John shook hands with the stunning man in the back seat. Dark brown eyes under feathered black eyebrows gazed back at him while plump lips parted in a gleaming smile. "Thank you for all you have done for us," he said, his voice low and melodious.

"No problem." John backed out of the parking space and headed for the exit, keeping an eye out between the rows of parked cars for anyone else trying to get in their way. "So, the guy with the sign. You reckon he's with the religious sect you mentioned on the phone?"

John caught sight of Jareem nodding vigorously in his rear-view mirror while Sam replied, "Definitely. They've been after Jareem for close to a year. Thanks to his many friends in Kabul, he's managed to stay under the radar, but a month ago one of his friends inadvertently let it slip to Jareem's father that he'd seen him in Darulaman, outside Kabul. He managed to get in touch with me and explained the situation, saying he'd have to move again."

"My father would've sent his lackeys to find me and take me home," Jareem told him. "He has vowed to use his right of honor killing if I do not renounce my sexuality and marry the woman of their choice."

"Honor killing?" John met Jareem's gaze in the mirror.

"He says I have brought shame to our family because of my love for Samuel."

"Honor killing is illegal in Afghanistan," Sam said, turning so that he could take Jareem's hand. "But that doesn't stop it from being carried out, unfortunately, and the family members are rarely punished for the crime. Most honor killings are against women, but it has been known for young gay men to be targeted. I think what compounded Jareem's father's anger is the fact that I'm an American. No way could he allow this to go unpunished. When Jareem told me of his father's threat, I knew I had to get him out of there. There is no protection for gay men and women in Afghanistan."

"Well, like I said, I'm glad you made it here safely." John took the exit ramp for North Hollywood, staying alert in case anyone might be tailing them. But with the amount of traffic on LA freeways, it was near impossible. "Now, all we have to do is make sure those thugs don't get near you. Our house is secure, has a state-of-the-art alarm system and Mark and I are both armed, plus he'll have a patrol detail set up while you're with us. I'm guessing you'll both want to catch some zees."

Sam nodded. "We were sleeping pretty rough the last few days. We had cots at the military base before we left, which were better than a cement floor, but I'd give my arm for a comfy bed."

"That we can give you, and I don't need your arm." John chuckled at his joke and Jareem joined in, but Sam stared straight ahead, looking grim. Jareem rested his hands on Sam's shoulders and massaged them gently.

"Sorry." Sam gripped one of Jareem's hands and kissed it. "I can't get around the fact that my own father refused to help us. We've had our differences in the past, but I thought that maybe, just maybe, he'd come through in this instance, knowing how dangerous Jareem's situation was. If it hadn't been for Mrs. Melville's intervention, God only knows where we'd have ended up."

"Yeah, it was kind of a surprise when Millie, my secretary, told me she knew Mrs. Melville from her time in the diplomatic service." John chuckled. "I didn't know I had such influential friends. Anyway, I know you only asked for a couple of nights, but I think after what we witnessed at the airport, you need to stay until you find somewhere secure."

John knew that decision would not go down well with Millie. He also knew her disapproval came from concern for Mark and himself, but sometimes risks had to be taken to keep people safe. Somehow, the obvious affection Sam and Jareem had for each other had brought out his protective instincts, and he'd really hate to see something bad happen to either one of them. Sam looked like he could take care of himself. He noticed the chest and biceps that strained under Sam's shirt. The guy was fit, but if Jareem's father had hired trained killers or kidnappers, it would take more than just physical ability to get them out of trouble.

He took another look in his rear-view mirror as they cruised onto the quiet street where he and Mark lived. *Looks as if the coast is clear,* he thought, with a grateful sigh. But, just in case… He drove to the end of the street, turned right then circled around, constantly looking out for any suspicious car following them.

Finally satisfied, he pulled into their garage and closed the door before getting out of the car.

"Okay, guys, grab your stuff and let me give you the grand tour."

Jareem shot him a dazzling smile. *He really is a beauty, and amazingly calm considering what he's been through.* John punched in the code to release the alarm and opened the door for them. "Straight through to the living room. Can I get you something to eat or drink?"

"Just some cold water for me," Sam said, while Jareem nodded his agreement. "Is there a shower to go with the bed?"

"You bet." He handed them a bottle of water each. "Let me show you the spare bedroom." They followed him down the hall and he pointed out the bathroom on the way. "I've put clean towels out and stuff you'll need, and here's your own hideaway. I'll leave you both to do your thing. If you need anything, just shout. I'll be here, and Mark gets home around six."

"Thank you," Jareem said, giving John a little bow. "We appreciate everything you have done for us."

"Just relax as much as you can. Shower, sleep. We'll have something to eat when you surface. Take as long as you need."

"Thanks, John." Sam's voice was gruff. John intuited that as much as Sam welcomed the help, he was already looking at ways to ensure Jareem's safety permanently, just as he or Mark would do for each other.

"See you later." He closed the door and went back to the living room. He palmed his cell phone and speed-dialed Mark. "Hi, lover. They're here and I got them to the house safely. I did a circular tour to get to the house just in case we were being followed." He recounted what had happened at LAX.

"How in hell did they know what flight the guys would be on?" Mark rasped.

"Someone must have spilled the beans. From what I gather, Jareem knows a lot of people in Kabul, some his friends, but some obviously not." He told Mark about the honor killing threat.

"Jesus, we need to get them to a safe house. No way can we afford to have paid thugs show up at our house."

"Yeah, what would the neighbors say?"

Mark's chuckle was dry. "Looks like we'll have to get the FBI involved, dammit." He heaved a loud sigh. "Okay, I should be home around six. I'll have a patrol car cruise the neighborhood in the meantime. And, John, please be careful. Make sure the alarm is on, even when you're home."

"Yes, sir."

"Don't be a smartass. Just be careful."

"I will. Love you."

"Love you too."

Chapter Nine

He'd hung up before he remembered to ask if there had been any news about Alex. *That guy has gone totally off the rails,* he thought as he prepared a sandwich for himself. A sandwich he could do without a lot of trouble. Long as he used lots of mayo and mustard, the generally tasteless processed meats were okay.

Wonder where he is? And is he ever gonna turn himself in? Mark would go easy on him if he made the first move, but this constant on-the-run thing he was doing would not go over well, even with Mark.

He poured himself a glass of sparkling water then sat at the kitchen table ready to devour his sandwich. He looked up as Sam came into the kitchen. "Couldn't sleep?"

"Nothing against your very comfortable bed, but my mind's going a thousand miles an hour."

"Jareem sleeping?"

"Like the proverbial log, I'm happy to say."

"Can I fix you a sandwich?"

"No thanks. We did have something execrable on the plane. I'm too keyed up to eat, but thank you again. Perhaps some water?"

"Sure. Sparkling or regular?"

"Regular's fine. One doesn't appreciate the wonder of clean, bottled water until you've tasted what the poor people in Afghanistan have to put up with." He accepted the bottle John handed him. "So you're Native American, John?"

"Yes. Dakota Sioux. My mother still lives on the Pine Ridge reservation in South Dakota."

"What's her name?"

"Kimimela… It means butterfly."

Sam nodded. "Pretty. She chose an Anglican name for you, John."

"Yes, she said, when I was ready to leave the reservation, I should have a name that people didn't stumble over." John smiled. "My grandmother called me Kohana. It means swift. She said she never saw a two-year-old run as fast as I did."

"And your father?"

"I never knew him, but my mom told me he was of the tribe…and very handsome."

Sam smiled. "Like father, like son."

"Thanks, but I hope I'm a better man than he was. Leaving a young wife and newborn was cruel and, in a way, cowardly."

"Can't argue with that, but you seem to have come out of it very well."

John nodded. "My mother and grandmother set me on the right path. After my father deserted us, my mother and grandmother raised me. They taught me to respect the tribal traditions. I had an uncle who would take me on tracking and hunting expeditions. As a kid

I thought it was all a game, and fun, but it's a time I've never forgotten."

"I bet. A lot of kids would love that kind of upbringing. Did school get in the way?"

"Not really. There were still the weekends and the holidays. In high school I won a scholarship to SDU."

"What did you major in?"

"Marine biology, but I'm afraid the urge to do something more exciting lured me to Hollywood, working as an extra in movies. I had visions of one day being the next Michael Greyeyes. Then I met Mark and my life changed again…for the better."

"How did you two meet?" Sam asked.

John chuckled. "Not in the traditional way, that's for sure." He went on to explain how he'd been set up by Greg Mathis then arrested and interrogated by Mark.

"Greg Mathis?" Sam frowned at the end of John's story. "Can't say I know the name."

"He was big for a while, then he wasn't." John shrugged. "The price you pay for dealing with lowlifes, I guess." They were silent for a few moments while John tackled his sandwich, until he asked, "Have you spoken to your sister since you've been back?"

"Yes, I called her soon as we landed. She sounded…fatalistic, I suppose is the best way to describe it. She's never approved of my being bisexual. Then again, she didn't care for my ex-wife. When I told her about Jareem, she had a fit…said I was ruining my life and would probably get myself in a lot of trouble if I didn't drop him immediately—and never go back to Afghanistan."

"Well, she was right about the trouble. How did you guys meet?"

"At a diplomatic function. I was there with members of a peacekeeping team." He laughed self-consciously. "At the risk of sounding like a total cliché, I saw him and it was as if the room held only the two of us. I couldn't have stayed away from him if there had been wild horses holding me back. I had to meet him…and I did. Brazenly, I might add. Ignoring all the protocols of foreign diplomacy, I marched over to where he was standing talking with two other men, introduced myself and asked him if he'd like to get a breath of fresh air."

"Fast mover," John said, grinning.

Sam laughed. "More like pushy, and I braced myself expecting him to say no, but he took my arm and we went outside on the veranda. We talked, and I was enchanted from the get-go. Well, you've seen him, right? But it was more than just his looks. There was…is…an air about him that I find irresistible. He's intelligent, kind. He has a purity of soul so at odds with the conflict around him…and his family. He hates what is happening in his country, the government corruption, the terrorism, the lack of leadership, the poverty that afflicts so many Afghanis.

"We arranged to meet, in secret of course, and he enlisted the help of a friend to make that happen. I knew I was taking a chance, but I really didn't think that the fallout would be as terrible as it was for him. On our third time together, or rather it would have been the third time, he wasn't at his friend's house. Some men had shown up, his friend told me, and taken him. His father had instigated it. He is a monster. Jareem's brother followed the old man's instructions to have it appear as if Jareem had been kidnapped. Feisal, the brother, turned a blind eye when Jareem was flogged."

"All because he's gay?"

"That, and being in the company of an infidel. Believe me, John, hatred for the Western world is still very much a part of their culture. We are not loved by Islam."

"I spoke with Ellis Watkins, who was on the team with you. He said you put yourself in danger rescuing Jareem."

"Well, I went a bit berserk when I found out what had happened to him. We'd only just met, I was falling for him and suddenly he'd been torn from me. I wasn't going to stand for that." He fell silent for a moment, as if remembering the danger Jareem had been in. "Jareem's friends told me where he'd been taken. It's true I was probably reckless, but I prefer to think the thugs were caught by surprise and that made it easy for me to get to Jareem and set him free."

John figured Sam was downplaying his part in the rescue, and that made him admire the man even more.

"Then of course," Sam continued, "I couldn't take him back to the States, no matter how many strings I tried to pull through the peacekeeping group. I appealed to the UN, to the embassy, but his father was just too powerful, so I had to come back alone. At least his family took him in when he got out of the hospital, on condition that he forget all about me and marry a woman. Any woman, I suppose, preferably of their choosing. After several months, I was able to communicate with him by phone and internet. I managed to get a visa so I could travel to Kabul. It was risky, but for me it was worth it, just to see him again. We met at a friend's home."

"And this last time?" John prompted. "Your sister said Jareem was in hiding."

"Yes, another friend, Abdul, took him in. Jareem's father had become even more overbearing, demanding Jareem marry, and so he slipped out of the house to stay with his friend Abdul. But it became too dangerous, too hard for his friend to keep denying Jareem's presence. Abdul contacted me and more or less said I had to get Jareem out of the country or he would be killed once his family found him."

"Hard to believe that a father would feel so little for his son," John said bitterly.

"Not really." Sam shrugged. "I believe that if I were in dire straits, my father would be the last to help me. He threatened to kill me once."

"What the hell could bring him to threaten you like that?"

"Let's just say that his business ethics are at odds with mine and he didn't like me pointing it out. He and some of our shareholders wanted to approve a loan program that was attractive to low-wage earners but had a hidden balloon payment due in three years. I blew up at him over it, more or less accusing him of usury. He went nuts. His threats to kill me came in the heat of the verbal brawl we got into, but from the anger he displayed, I thought he just might try to do it.

"Once he'd calmed down and seemed to realize he'd been overreacting, he gave me a half-assed apology, which I didn't for a moment believe was sincere. I knew he and I were never going to get along, but for me it was easier to pretend his words weren't as dangerous as they seemed, although Penny made a big deal out of it. However, his actions when I asked Penny to have him contact his senator friend for help spoke volumes.

He really couldn't give a shit about me. He and I will probably never speak to each other again."

"Doesn't that make working with him kinda awkward?"

"It would be all kinds of awkward if I continued working there, but I intend to resign from the company. I make enough money on my lecture tours to keep Jareem and me in comfort. All I want to do is hold him close, keep him safe."

John nodded. "We have something in common. That's how I feel about Mark. As a cop, he's been in the danger zone a few times…more than a few, really, and I just pray each time that he'll come through it safe so that I can…like you said, hold him close and thank the gods he's still with me."

Sam smiled. "It's great that you both have such a connection. That's what I'm hoping for Jareem and me, once we get through this mess." It looked as if he was fighting a yawn, then had to give in. "Wow, I think maybe I should try to get some sleep after all. It suddenly caught up with me."

"Go right ahead. I'll wake you when it's time for dinner." *Whatever that might be…*

"Sounds good." Sam rose from his chair. "Thanks for letting me bend your ear."

"No problem. See you later."

"Right, later."

John carried his plate and glass into the kitchen then busied himself tidying up. His cell chimed with a call from Mark. "Hey, husband, what's up?"

Mark's voice was grim. "Sorry, John, I have some bad news."

"Tell me."

"Alex…he's dead. His body was found in the trunk of his car. It had been abandoned off the freeway near La Cienega. Stan and Brett have the body and forensics is going over his car even as we speak. We won't know anything for a while, but I'll keep you apprised when I get something. Sorry to give you this news, but when he didn't show up the second time around, I had a feeling something bad had happened."

"Yeah…shit." John squeezed his eyes tight. *Poor Alex.* "You think the boyfriend had something to do with it?"

"Too early. There's an APB out on him and we're checking up on any associates of his. I'm still thinking about Alex's story about there being two other guys in the park when Forsythe was killed." He paused, then asked, "How're Sam and Jareem?"

"Asleep. Sam and I talked for a while about the situation in Afghanistan, but I'll fill you in on that later. Will you still be coming home at six, or later?"

"I might still make it by six. If there's no news from the coroner's office, I can pick it up tomorrow."

"Okay. I was thinking of ordering in pizzas for us."

"Good idea. Make it Round Table…there's one near the house. Have them deliver after six, but if I'm not home I'll have a black and white outside, just in case."

John sighed. "I think we should go on vacation after all this is over. Just you and me and an ocean view."

"We just got back from Hawaii, John," Mark said, chuckling.

"Wow, that seems a long time ago."

"It does, but it's gonna have to do until I can get more time off, and you know what that's like."

John was depressed after he and Mark disconnected their call. Like he'd told Mark, he and Alex hadn't been close friends, but he couldn't deny the pervading sense of loss, nevertheless. It was rough to imagine the big guy, or at least as John had once known him back in the day, full of fun and raunchiness, discarded as if his life had meant nothing, in the trunk of his car. He remembered how they'd laughed when they'd shared some of their stories about working with some of the major stars. One story he'd told John had been about working with an aging movie star on a TV series about the old west.

"Jeff Williams was still a big star at the time, had been for years, so everyone was kinda in awe of him. I guess I was too, and pumped because I had a scene with him. I was this Indian stoking up a fire, supposedly to send smoke signals. Then he comes out of the rocks, charging at me. I jumped to my feet to grapple with him and the fucker stuck his leg between mine, rubbing up into my crotch. I was wearing one of those flimsy breechclout thingies and of course I got hard. I was young and got instant hard-ons, you know like you do. Didn't matter who or what was doing the rubbing.

"Anyway, the director yelled cut and said something about fixing the sound. I can't remember what. But the old guy didn't move back, just kept on rubbing, watching my expression, probably getting off himself. Then when the director said that it was going to take longer than he thought, the old fucker just patted my face, chuckled and walked away. I had to run behind one of the rocks with my hands over my crotch till I cooled down. Every time he looked at me after that he had a stupid smirk on his face like 'wanna go again'? Of course I didn't."

They'd laughed together, but truth was that it had reminded John of the time when Greg Mathis had more or less acted that same way…except John had accepted the invitation to go again, and had almost ended up in jail for the mistake. The only good thing out of the whole scenario was that he'd met Mark, but it still made him shudder sometimes when he thought that it all could've gone so very wrong. Especially when the DNA match seemed to have damned him as the murderer. Only Mark's belief in him had gotten him through that terrible time.

* * * *

Sam and Jareem joined him in the living room later, and Sam was enthusiastic about having pizza for dinner.

"Haven't had one in ages," he remarked. "I'm always so damn healthy food conscious, but after what we've been through, I think pizza is the best celebratory food we could have."

"I have never had a pizza," Jareem said, "but from the look of expectation on your face, I know I will like it."

John chuckled. "Wow, hard to believe a person has never eaten a pizza. Mark and I are both such lousy cooks we have it at least once a week. Thin crust or thick?"

"Thin, of course. Nice and crispy." Sam rubbed his hands together.

"Toppings?" John asked.

"Anything but pineapple."

"Ugh." John made a face. "And anchovies."

"I like anchovies," Jareem said.

"Honey…" Sam gave his lover a solemn look. "Lips that touch anchovies will never touch mine."

John choked back a laugh. "Well, we can't have that!"

"Okay, no anchovies." Jareem's laughter was contagious, and they were still laughing when Mark walked into the room.

"What'd I miss?"

"Hey." John hugged him. "Want you to meet Sam and Jareem. Guys, this is my husband, Mark."

Sam was the first to cross over to them and hold out his hand. "So pleased to meet you, Mark, and to say thank you in person for all you're doing for us."

"Well, John has told me what you guys have been going through," Mark said, shaking Sam's hand. "So this is the least we can do for you."

Jareem approached Mark and bowed, his hands clasped to his chest. "Thank you," he said softly. His dark eyes appraised Mark's face and body. "You and John are beautiful men."

"Thank you, Jareem." Mark's face pinked, much to John's amusement.

"So…" John grinned at his husband. "I'll order the pizzas. Why don't you get some drinks for our guests?"

"Oh yeah, sure. Beers all around, or we do have wine?"

"Beer would be great," Sam said. "For me. Jareem doesn't drink alcohol."

"How about some sparkling water?" Mark offered.

"That would be very nice, thank you," Jareem replied.

Wow. John punched in the number for the pizza place. *Jareem is Mr. Manners all right.* After he'd placed the order, he walked into the kitchen, where Mark and Sam were drinking their beer and Jareem was perched on a bar stool, a small frown on his pretty face.

Mark looked at John as he joined the group. "I was explaining to Sam and Jareem that the best thing for them would be a safe house rather than them looking for an apartment. I talked to the chief and he agreed. Soon as one becomes available, he'll let me know. Till then, it'd be best if they stay with us, but we're gonna have to limit their movement—"

"In other words, we're to stay indoors," Sam said with some bitterness.

"'Fraid so," Mark replied. "But it'll only be a few days. I'm pretty sure we can find you somewhere safe by then."

"I have lectures to give," Sam told him. "That is my career and I'm not willing to give that up right now. If I start canceling dates at short notice, it will mar my reputation. I can't afford that."

"I could go with you," John said. "Watch your back, keep an eye out for anything or anyone suspicious."

Mark sighed. "John, this is a police operation, and tomorrow, the FBI will be involved because of the international connections. Regardless of the help you received from the embassy, there are still bad guys out there wanting to do you and Jareem harm…and, most likely, take Jareem back to his family. When is your first lecture?" he asked Sam.

"In two weeks, at the Irvine campus. They usually arrange for hotel accommodations for me for the night. I suppose that'll be out too."

Mark nodded. "The FBI will have talked with you by then. For your and Jareem's safety, you'll have to do what they require."

Sam grimaced. "You're right, of course. Jareem's safety is paramount. Sorry if I sounded pissy. Guess the last few days have gotten to me."

"Understandable." Mark patted Sam's shoulder lightly. "The FBI said they'd send their agents out tomorrow. We're to meet them at the precinct at eleven a.m., so we just have to stay vigilant until then, decide what's the best way to keep you safe."

"I would like it if Sam and I could stay with you both," Jareem said softly. "I feel safe here."

Sam put his arm around Jareem and kissed his cheek. "I'd like that too, babe, but until we're out of the woods, we have to do whatever law enforcement mandates."

John could tell from the look of compassion on his husband's face that he wished he could do more for the guys. That was one of the many reasons he loved Mark. He was a tough cop with a heart, and if he could, he'd make sure Sam and Jareem's future was, at the very least, a safe one. But right now, he had to go by the book, and the chief had obviously gotten the FBI involved, so that was that.

The doorbell chimed. "That'll be the pizza guy." He made for the door and suddenly Mark was at his side, his gun drawn, one arm covering John's chest.

"I said be careful, didn't I?"

"Sorry."

Mark checked the screen above the door. "He *looks* like a pizza guy." Mark holstered his Beretta, disengaged the alarm and opened the door.

"Hi." The fresh-faced kid gave him a big smile. "Order for Mr. White Eagle. Is that your real name?"

"No, it's his." He opened the door slightly wider so the kid could see John standing next to him.

"Cool name." He handed over the boxes. "That'll be forty dollars." John paid him and added a tip. "Wow, thanks." The kid smiled and turned to go. "Have a good evening, guys."

"You too." John closed the door and reset the alarm. "There's a black and white on the other side of the street."

"I noticed. Okay, let's eat. I am starving."

"Smells great," Sam said.

"Okay, everyone dig in." John laid the boxes on the kitchen table. Mark got some more beers from the fridge, and as they sat at the table, John couldn't help but think this was almost like any other night they'd spent with friends. Pizza and beer and conversation. Maybe a game of cards. Except this night wasn't like any other. Mark taking his gun out when he'd answered the door had been a reminder of that. Sam and Jareem weren't their friends…at least, not yet. They were two men on the run from a vicious family who'd hired thugs to either take them out or take Jareem home to be suitably punished.

As hard as it was for John to understand that part, he knew it existed. He knew that Sam and Jareem's lives were in danger, no matter how 'normal' this little scene suggested it was. Gazing across the table at Sam chowing down on his pizza and Jareem more delicately nibbling at the crisp bread, a sense of urgency gripped him. No matter what, he and Mark would protect this likeable, intelligent man and his sweet-faced lover. For as long as Sam and Jareem were with them, it was his and Mark's duty to keep them out of harm's way and be forever alert to the possible danger outside.

Chapter Ten

Sam closed the door to the guest room quietly and smiled at Jareem. He opened his arms and Jareem moved swiftly into his embrace. Their kiss was long and sweet, but with an underlying degree of impatient lust. It had been several days since they'd last made love and the way their bodies were reacting to each other was proof of that.

"Samuel," Jareem gasped after he drew a shaky breath. "Thank you for caring so much that you would risk everything for me."

"I would do it over and over," Sam whispered. "And now that we're at last alone, just you and me and that rather nice-looking bed, would you let me express just how much I love you?"

Jareem's smile was everything to Sam. For three years, he had longed for a time like this, when they could hold each other without fear of being discovered and forced apart. He gazed at Jareem's face, at the smooth planes of his cheeks, the dark brown eyes beneath feathered eyebrows, those eyes that gazed back at him filled with so much love... *For me,* Sam exulted...and that mouth so full and sinfully lush, made to be kissed over and over. He could look at Jareem forever and never tire of his beauty. As for kissing...

Jareem moved to the bed and sat on the edge, removing his shirt as he gazed at Sam, his smile now tantalizingly sexy. Sam stripped quickly, leaving only his briefs on, then helped Jareem with his shoes and socks, kneeling before him to tug them off, lifting each foot to kiss it gently. Jareem ran his fingers through Sam's hair and leaned forward to kiss Sam's forehead.

"*Dostat daaram,*" he said softly. "So much, Sam."

"I love you, too, my angel..."

Sam stepped out of his briefs. He pushed Jareem gently onto his back, lying over him, grinding their bodies together with slow, sensual moves, claiming him again with a deep kiss of longing that had them both gasping into each other's mouths. Sam trailed kisses down to the hollow beneath Jareem's throat, sucking on it gently before tracing a sensual pattern over Jareem's chest with his lips, settling on each nipple to lick and tease and nibble.

Jareem moaned and squirmed under him, thrusting his groin into Sam's, rubbing their erections together, letting Sam feel the slickness of their shared pre-cum. "Will you fuck me, Sam?" Jareem asked softly. "It has been so long since I felt you inside me. Nothing brings me greater joy than for us to be joined as one."

"Willingly," Sam murmured. "And thanks to John, we have what we need. He left supplies in the bathroom for us, and I brought them in here."

"He is a good man," Jareem said, his eyes gleaming.

"He is." Sam kissed Jareem's lips, his throat, at the same time nudging his legs open. Sam reached for the lube and slicked Jareem's hole, pushing one then two fingers past his resistance. He was tight, and although Sam knew Jareem was eager to have Sam inside him, he didn't want their first time in so long to be unpleasant.

"I'll go slow," he whispered. "Tell me if it's uncomfortable."

Jareem stroked Sam's face. "The pain is nothing compared to the pleasure, *eshgham*."

Sam laid a soft kiss on Jareem's lips. *Eshgham*... He remembered the first time Jareem had called him *my love* in Afghani. He'd had to ask him what it meant, as no one had ever used the word in his presence before. It had been then that he'd fallen for the beautiful young man and had vowed that no matter what, they would live to spend the rest of their lives together.

He eased the condom over his already aching erection, then lifted Jareem's legs around his waist. He guided himself between Jareem's delectable ass cheeks, breaching him as gently as he could.

"More," Jareem urged, holding on to Sam's hips. "I will not break, *eshgham*. Fuck me." He wrapped his arms around Sam's neck and held him, shivering with ecstasy as Sam hit his prostate again and again with every one of his rhythmic thrusts. He arched into Sam's powerful body and Sam lifted him onto his lap, supporting him as he slid deeper inside him. Now they were chest to chest, lips to lips, and Sam wasted no time in claiming those luscious lips again. Their tongues glided and tangled together. Their combined moans echoed in Sam's brain. The sensual sounds encouraged him to drive harder and deeper into Jareem, who tightened his legs around Sam's hips and responded to each and every one of Sam's powerful thrusts with his own. The rhythm they'd found increased in momentum and Sam reveled in the rapture that making love to Jareem always brought him. And now, soon perhaps, they would no longer be pursued by those who could do them harm. All that existed for him was this one beautiful man who was clinging to him, kissing him like no other man ever had and taking this incredible, erotic journey along with him.

Jareem groaned, his body spasmed under Sam's and a creamy warmth spread between their tightly pressed torsos. Sam rammed himself into Jareem, his strokes faster, almost uncontrolled, as he neared his climax. Heat was centered at the bottom of his spine, inching its way into his balls. He wrenched his mouth away from Jareem's and let out a strangled cry of sheer ecstasy as he came, filling Jareem with his hot cum. Spent, he lowered Jareem back onto the mattress and lay over him, nuzzling the soft skin between his lover's neck and shoulder. Jareem licked the sweat from Sam's forehead and nibbled on his earlobe.

"*Dostat daaram,*" he murmured into the shell of Sam's ear.

"*Dostat daaram,*" Sam replied. "And I always will."

* * * *

John lay beside Mark, listening to the steady breathing that told him his husband was asleep. He wished he could join him, but sleep didn't seem to be on the horizon any time soon. Usually, after sex, he was ready for a sleepy snuggle, but tonight he was decidedly restless.

Something didn't feel right. That knot in the pit of his stomach told him so. He might have downplayed Mark's opinion that he'd been imbued with some kind of sexual voodoo, but his innate knack for knowing when something was off had helped him out of some tight spots in the past. He slipped out of the bed, unwilling to disturb Mark by tossing and turning for what could be hours if he couldn't calm his mind down some. Putting on his discarded boxers, he left the bedroom then padded silently down the hall into the living room, where he sat on his favorite chair by the window.

It had been a day, without a doubt. Sam and Jareem were safe, for now, and once the FBI stepped in, he and Mark could most likely take a back seat in the operation. Alex's death troubled him, though. The guy had come to him for help with a situation that had gotten out of hand. That shouldn't have happened. Whoever had killed Donald Forsythe, Alex's blackmailer, had to be tied to Alex's death somehow. John was convinced of that.

He was distracted by a movement over by the black and white on the other side of the street. Someone was standing outside the car talking to the cops inside. John stood to get a better look at what was going on. Another man approached the patrol car and, to John's amazement, tried to open the door. He could hear shouting now. *Shit, what the hell?* The car door swung open and a shot rang out. The officer who'd been about to heave himself out of his seat fell back inside.

Fuck... He ran back down the hall to the bedroom. "Mark, wake up, quick. There's a problem outside. One of the officers has been shot."

Mark was out of the bed instantly, grabbing for his briefs and pants. John threw him his shoulder holster and picked up his own gun and cell phone from the nightstand. A crash from the vicinity of the front of the house and the shrieking of the alarm told them the door had been battered in.

"Tell Sam and Jareem to stay in their room," Mark yelled as he charged into the hall, gun in both hands, aimed and ready to fire. The ear-splitting sounds of rapid-fire shots echoed through the house, and as John barged into the guestroom, he heard a heavy thump then someone cry out in pain.

Not Mark… No time to feel relieved, though.

"What's happening?" Sam was pulling on his briefs while Jareem stared at John with wide, terrified eyes.

"Stay here until I tell you to come out. I mean it," he added as Sam made a move toward him. He pulled the door closed and inched his way down to the living room, his back pressed to the hallway wall. There was a body on the floor. Mark was standing in the doorway and John joined him, watching in disbelief as the patrol car sped off down the street. The officer John had seen shot was stretched out in the road.

"I winged one of them," Mark said. "Check to see if that one's alive." He jerked his head toward the prone thug on the living room floor. "Tie him up if he is. I'm calling for backup. You call nine-one-one for an ambulance." He set off to check on the fallen officer.

John rolled the thug onto his back. No need to check for a pulse. His dead eyes stared back at John. A hole in his forehead oozed blood.

Sam came into the room, followed by Jareem holding tight to Sam's hand. They'd gotten dressed in shorts and T-shirts. "What the fuck?" Sam muttered.

"Looks like at least one of the cops watching the house was not on our side…or the other gunman has him as hostage." He got up and punched in the emergency number. "Yeah, need an ambulance to ninety-nine Fennel Road, North Hollywood. Police officer has been shot. And we have one dead suspect. Okay." He hung up and stared at Sam. "Your enemies are too damned stupid by half."

They both turned when Mark entered the house, supporting the officer who John had seen shot. He was young and pale and bleeding from his shoulder. Mark lowered him carefully onto a chair and started to remove his jacket.

"Get me a towel, John, so we can stanch the blood. Medics on their way?"

"Yes." He ran to the linen closet and yanked out a towel. When he got back, Mark had opened the young cop's shirt and was examining the wound on his shoulder.

"Not too bad, Officer Randall," Mark told him. "The bullet missed the important stuff. Now, you wanna tell me who your partner is and what he was doing?"

Randall gazed at Mark through teary eyes. "Kyle Brenton. The bastard set me up, I guess. Told me to get out of the car and let them do their job. I didn't know what he was talking about. 'What job?' I asked." He winced when Mark pressed the towel over the wound. "Kyle just nodded over at your place, then he said, 'Don't get in the way and you'll be all right.' I said no way, I was calling it in. He punched me on the back of the head and opened the door. He said, 'Sorry, Mike, this'll hurt,' and the guy standing there shot me. I must've blacked out, because next thing I know, you're asking me if I can walk…"

"So we can't even trust the police," Sam said bitterly.

"We must go." Jareem tugged on Sam's arm. "We are putting too many people's lives in danger."

"You're not going anywhere," Mark told him. A siren's wail sounded, coming closer. "Go sit at the table so we can talk once the medics have taken care of Randall here, and…" He flicked a disgusted look at the dead man. "Whoever that is. No I.D., John?"

"None. We'll have to wait for the coroner's report."

"*You* killed him?" Jareem asked.

Mark nodded. "I wounded one of the others as well. Kyle Brenton will be apprehended shortly." Mark shook his head. "Goddam fool and a total amateur. The only way he could have gotten away with it was to have killed us all. He really fucked up."

"And for that we are all truly thankful," John said wryly.

Four paramedics suddenly piled into the house. John watched as Mark informed them what had happened then spoke with the police officers who had followed them in. He went back to their bedroom, grabbed T-shirts for Mark and himself then sat at the table with Sam and Jareem.

"You holding up all right?"

Sam nodded, but Jareem was staring at the activity in the room, worrying his lower lip with his teeth. Sam took his hand. "It'll be okay, Jareem. They'll find out who's behind this and put them behind bars."

"If Mark doesn't shoot them first," John said, chuckling.

"I suppose this kind of thing doesn't faze you guys one bit," Sam said, stroking the back of Jareem's hand with his thumb.

"I wouldn't say that exactly, but Mark has been on the force for fifteen years, so he's been around enough bad guys to give him an edge when it comes to dealing with them."

"He is very brave," Jareem said with quiet admiration.

John couldn't help noticing that Jareem was crushing on Mark. Not a good idea, although he couldn't blame him. Mark was a hot cop and all business when the need arose, like defending his home, and now, giving the officers a rundown of what had taken place.

"We think," he said with a glance John's way, "that these guys were hired by Jareem's father to either bring him home or kill him. FBI agents have been informed and are supposedly contacting me tomorrow."

Two paramedics were finishing up attending to Randall while the other two lifted the dead thug's body onto a gurney and wheeled him out.

"So, Jareem." John thought he might have to snap his fingers to get the young man's attention away from Mark, but he turned and met John's gaze with a small smile. "Did you know that your father had connections with the Los Angeles Police Department?"

Jareem shook head. "No, but my father is a very powerful man with connections in many places and with many people, so it is not surprising to me that one of the would-be killers was a policeman. In Kabul, the chief of police is a good friend of my father's."

Sam gave a nod of agreement. "He has fingers everywhere, but not just him. Many wealthy families between them control the police and, in some cases, sections of the military. Not very much goes on that they don't know about. I truly did not believe that we would get away, even with your friend's help…until the moment we boarded the plane for New York."

"And yet they had managed a welcome for you at LAX."

Sam frowned. "Yes, I didn't expect them to move so quickly…and now this." He sighed. "Jareem is right. We need to leave before anyone else on our side gets hurt."

"You need to be in a safe house," John said firmly. "Not some apartment that can be breached even more easily than our house. A safe place no one knows where you are. So no trying to leave here until Mark or the FBI gets that fixed up for you. We just have to be vigilant at all times."

They watched as Randall was taken away by the medics and Mark walked his fellow officers to the door. "They're gonna set up another patrol for us," he said when he joined them at the table. "And sending someone over to plug up the door for the night."

John reached over and rubbed Mark's shoulder, telling himself he wasn't staking his claim for Jareem to see…but he was really. He didn't want the cute guy thinking he could thank Mark in a special way when no one else was around. He was probably overreacting, but still…

"I think you guys should get some shut-eye," Mark said. "It'll be a busy day tomorrow, or should I say later this morning? I'll sit out here until the repairmen come to fix the door."

"I'll stay with you," John said. "Sam and Jareem should get some sleep, though."

"Don't think I could sleep a wink." Sam stretched and yawned mightily. "But there I go, making a liar out of myself. Come on, babe." He stood and took Jareem's hand, coaxing him gently to his feet. "We'll get out of your hair for now. Sorry for bringing all this trouble, literally, to your front door."

"No problem. Get some rest and we'll talk more tomorrow." Mark sighed when his cell rang. "Rossi." His forehead creased as he listened to whoever was on the line. "Okay, I'll meet with the chief first thing tomorrow."

He disconnected the call. "That was the duty officer at the precinct. Officer Kyle Brenton was found shot dead in the patrol car. It was parked on La Brea. No sign of the other guy, but there was blood on the passenger seat. Could be he was the one I got with my second shot. Wounded at least, but not enough to stop him getting away."

"You think he shot Brenton?" John asked.

"Who else could it have been? Unless there was someone else waiting at a predetermined meeting place with their backup, but that doesn't seem likely as the car was left in plain sight."

"But why kill the police officer?" Sam asked.

Mark shrugged. "He might've panicked, seeing his partner getting shot, then the raid on our house going so wrong for them. Who knows? I'm more interested in knowing why he was involved in the first place…and if there's anyone else in the force of like mind."

John nodded. "We have to make sure Sam and Jareem's future place is top secret."

"That'll be up to the FBI when we see the agents tomorrow. Right…let's call it a day. Sam, I'll wake you both when it's time for us to head to the precinct. Try to get some sleep now."

"We'll try." Sam put his arm around Jareem's shoulders and pulled him into his side. "Goodnight, guys…and thanks again."

Jareem murmured goodnight and left with Sam, his arm around his lover's waist.

John rested his forehead on Mark's shoulder. "What a night."

Mark wrapped his arms around him. "A night to remember…for all the wrong reasons, unfortunately. The men should be here shortly to fix the door. Why don't you go lie down?"

"I'd rather stay with you, if you don't mind." He pressed himself farther into Mark's embrace. "Bad guys with guns always make me worry that they'll hurt you one day and—"

Mark leaned back and tapped the tip of John's nose with his forefinger. "None of that morbid stuff. We both know what's out there and the chances we take. You as well as me. Don't you think I worry about you too? But life is full of chances, babe. Somebody said, you just have to roll with them—and watch your ass when you do!"

John chuckled and slid his hands over his husband's round muscular butt. "Mmm… Rather watch your ass any day." He kissed Mark's neck. "Love you so much."

"Love you too."

A truck pulling up outside had them stepping back with rueful smiles. "Just hold that thought for later," Mark whispered, then went to let the repairmen in.

Chapter Eleven

The federal agents were already in the meeting room, along with Mark's immediate supervisor, Chief Harlan Oates. The agents were cordial enough and introduced themselves as Agents Kenneth Henderson and Chris Wallace. Henderson, the older of the two, and ruggedly handsome, seemed like a nice enough guy. John wasn't so sure about the younger Wallace, who had thrown John a look that wasn't exactly friendly. After the introductions were over, Henderson signaled that they should all sit.

Wallace scrutinized John from pale blue eyes that held a hostile gleam. "Can I ask why there's a private detective at this meeting? What does he have to do with this case?"

Chief Oates cleared his throat irritably before he replied, "It's my understanding that John is the one who first made contact with Mr. Andrews and subsequently, with help from a member of the diplomatic corps, was able to assist Mr. Andrews and Mr. Durani to leave Afghanistan. That being the case, he was able to give us important information that might help us with the situation."

"Impressive," Wallace murmured with a trace of snark.

"Not really," John said, keeping his annoyance out of his voice. If Wallace wanted to be a prick, he could kiss John's ass. "Just so happens that my secretary knows people in very useful places. She and Audrey Melville, a retired diplomat, did all the *impressive* stuff."

Sam, sitting next to John, stirred. "That's true, and Jareem and I are, of course, immensely grateful to both ladies. And also to John and Mark for their quick actions which saved Jareem and myself last night. God knows where we'd be right now if not for them. We still feel terrible about their home being attacked last night by would-be killers."

Wallace remained impassive and silent, for which John was grateful. Any more snarky remarks from the agent and he might just have to shut his mouth down.

"D'you have all the facts on the case?" Mark asked Henderson.

The agent nodded. "Mr. Durani sought asylum at the embassy in Kabul, afraid that his father had threatened him with death by honor killing."

Wallace sighed. "Is that even likely?"

John stared at the agent. He really was proving himself to be a prick, and John's senses told him the man was a homophobe. "Why would you ask that? The threats to Jareem's life are very real, Agent. Jareem is in danger from his own family because he's gay, or is even that too hard for you to understand?"

Wallace bristled, but Sam diverted his attention away from John. "Honor killing is very real in certain Middle Eastern countries, Agent Wallace," he said quietly. "Jareem has been in hiding for several months with help from his friends. But even they can only help so much. They certainly didn't want to incur Jareem's father's wrath. Even though honor killing is officially banned, popular opinion is very much on his father's side, and only a few families are ever punished for the crime. That is why we had to leave. Jareem has been given a temporary passport, but we need the government's help to guarantee his safety while here in the States."

"What happened last night," Mark said, "was an indication that the thugs involved have good intel but are clumsy when it comes to carrying out orders."

"And they're not slow to punish those that let them down," Oates added. "One of our officers who was apparently aiding and abetting them ended up shot dead when the assassination attempt went wrong."

"No doubt they were afraid your officer would divulge information against them," Henderson said.

"Right." Mark pushed a folder across the table to Henderson. "Here's a complete report on what we have so far, including last night's incident and a statement from Officer Michael Randall, who was set up by his partner and shot. He's gonna be okay, by the way. What we need from you, asap, is a safe house for Sam and Jareem until we can be sure we've rounded up all the men involved, plus get assurances from Jareem's family that they will call off the honor killing."

"That will never happen," Jareem murmured sadly. "He will never forgive me. I am dead to him already."

"So why would he go through with killing you?" Wallace asked. His face was turned away, but John could practically hear the eye-roll. He really wanted to punch the guy's smug face. *What a dick.*

"Chris..." Henderson nudged Wallace's arm. "I think you're forgetting that different cultures have different rules. I was stationed in Afghanistan for two duty tours. They don't think like we do. Honor means...well, something different from how we see it." He turned to look at Sam and Jareem before saying, "We'll find you a safe place to stay while we and the police look for the men your father hired, and make sure they're imprisoned or deported."

"So..." Chief Oates got to his feet. "We'll leave them in your capable hands. Mark, I'll see you in my office when you're done here. Nice meeting you, gentlemen."

John wasn't at all sure about Chris Wallace's capable hands. He could tell the agent wasn't particularly on board with this assignment, and that worried John. If he was homophobic, as John suspected, or racist, or both, he was not going to be giving the situation his best shot.

Henderson was okay, he supposed, but he'd have been happier if both men had at least appeared to be in sync with each other. He wondered how long they'd been partnered. Not long, he figured, and although Henderson's rebuke had been mild, Wallace had still looked pissed at having been put in his place by the older agent.

"Okay, guys." Mark was on his feet and shaking hands with Sam.

John rose too and gave Jareem a smile of encouragement. The young Afghani placed his palms together and inclined his head toward John and Mark. As Wallace and Henderson gathered their things together, John whispered to Sam, "Call us when you're settled."

Sam nodded briefly. "Thanks for your help, both of you," he said, shaking John's hand.

After they'd left the room, John said, "I better let you get to your meeting with the chief."

"Yeah, he wants an update on Alex Vasquez's death, and right now I don't have one." He squeezed John's arm. "Don't look for me to be home early tonight. And keep the alarm on, okay?"

"Okay. I'll head over to the office. Millie called and said she'd be there to take messages, even though I said to let voicemail take them. Right now, I don't like the idea of her being there alone. Too many eyes."

"Know what you mean. Okay, I'll see you later."

"Later."

* * * *

Millie's smile when John entered the office seemed a tad forced, he thought. Certainly not the beaming one that usually greeted him.

"Hi, Millie, anything I should know about?"

"You look tired, John."

"Yeah, the past twenty-fours have been kinda hectic."

"I've been worried about you and Mark, and from the way you look, I think it was justified." She got up from her desk. "I'll brew some fresh coffee for you."

"You're a life-saver. The stuff they call coffee at the precinct should never see the light of day."

"So that's where you've been this morning?"

"Yep." As Millie busied herself at the coffee machine, he recounted the events of the previous day and night. "Just as well I couldn't sleep, or I might not have been able to alert Mark in time before they smashed the door in. Don't worry, we've had a brand-new door installed."

Millie shuddered. "I knew having Sam and Jareem at your house was a bad idea. But at least now the FBI have taken them off your hands."

"Yeah, just wish I felt better about that. One of the agents was a real winner. Young and full of smart-assery." John chuckled at Millie's raised eyebrows. "I know there's no such word, but it kinda suits him. His partner, Agent Henderson, was okay, but I told Sam when no one was listening to give me a call once they were settled in the safe house the FBI is providing."

"Should you get more involved, John?"

John sighed. "Probably not, but they're nice guys and could most likely use a friendly voice once in a while. By the way, once things are straightened out, they want to meet you and Mrs. Melville to say thanks properly."

"That's really not necessary."

"Maybe, but I think they'd like to meet you anyway. Oh…" His shoulders slumped a little. "You won't have heard about this. Bad news, I'm afraid. Yesterday, Alex was found dead in the trunk of his car."

"Oh, the poor man. Do the police have a suspect?"

"Not yet, but my money's on his boyfriend having something to do with it. Mark was in a meeting with Chief Oates when I left the precinct."

Millie poured John a mug of his favorite coffee. She looked at him and smiled as he groaned his pleasure when the aromatic brew met his taste buds. "Mmm, perfect as always. What did I do before you, Millie?"

"Managed quite well I suspect, and drank second-rate coffee."

They chuckled together, then John headed for his office. "I'm gonna do some research on Alex's boyfriend. See if I can come up with anything to help Mark." His cell chimed as he sat at his desk. "John White Eagle."

"Oh, hi, it's Penny, Sam's sister."

"Hi, Penny."

"I wondered how Sam was…and where he is. He's not answering his phone."

"He and Jareem are with FBI agents right now, Penny. They're going to a safe house…where, I don't know, I'm afraid. I guess he'll contact you at some point. I'm sure they're inundated with paperwork at the moment. It's a government thing, after all."

"How did he, uh, seem?"

"Quite well, considering what they've been through." He wasn't about to tell her about last night, but she ought to know the trouble her brother was in. "There are some pretty nasty types after them, trying to get Jareem back to his father—"

"Where he belongs," she said sharply.

"I was going to add 'or kill him'," John snapped. He was entirely over Penny Andrews. She was way too judgmental and not at all supportive of Sam…the brother she was so 'close' to. "They're not fussy which sentence they mete out. His father has decreed an honor killing as punishment for Jareem being gay and loving Sam. You still think he belongs back with a man who wants to see him dead?"

Penny sighed heavily. "Well, I suppose not. But I still don't quite see why he had to involve Sam in all of this."

"Sam is involved because he wants to be. He loves Jareem. I think his actions have proved that…to me, at least. I am sorry that you and your father don't approve of Sam's sexuality, but it really isn't either of your business. He is an adult and free to choose however he wants to live his life…and with whom."

"I see." Penny's tone was decidedly icy. "Well, thank you, Mr. White Eagle, for your candid opinion."

"You're welcome." John tried had to keep sarcasm out of his tone. "I'm sorry that things didn't turn out the way you wanted, but you must be happy that at least Sam is safe."

"Of course I am. Do I owe you any more money?"

"No. We're all square."

"Well then, goodbye, Mr. White Eagle."

"Goodbye, Miss Andrews." John shook his head as he placed his cell phone on his desk. He gazed through the open doorway at Millie, who was pretending not to have heard any of that conversation.

"So, what d'you think, Millie?" He got up and walked over to her desk.

"I think you handled that very well. Of course, I can only surmise what the young lady was saying, but judging by your responses, I would guess she is not happy with her brother's choice of boyfriend."

"She is not, and I'm afraid she's turned out to be a bit of a cold bitch."

Millie frowned. "Well, I did wonder about that when she tried to implicate her father in Sam's disappearance."

"Yeah, that was a strange thing for her to say. Sam did tell me his father's temper could be lethal. In the heat of the moment, he once threatened to kill Sam. He put it down to the man's temper and didn't think he'd actually do the deed. But he did say he wasn't surprised when his dad refused to help him get out of Afghanistan…angry, but not surprised."

"Not a happy family then," Millie said, her lips pursed. "What a terrible way to treat your son and daughter. Some people just shouldn't have children. Now, I think you and Mark would make wonderful fathers."

"Really? Don't you think our careers would make parenting difficult?"

"Well, I'd be happy to babysit for you should the need arise." She seemed to be warming to the subject as she continued, "You could check out adoption parameters, or even research surrogacy."

"Well, I'll have to talk this over with Mark."

"Oh, of course." She gave John a benign smile. "Something this important must be discussed mutually, and at length."

Chuckling, John walked back to his office. Mark and him as dads. They really hadn't thought of that very much, both of them being caught up with work and each other. *Maybe a puppy…*

He ran a background check on David Summers, looking for something that linked him to Donald Forsythe, the blackmailer. Both men had records. Was it possible they'd spent time in the same prison? He punched in Mark's number, hoping his meeting with the chief was over and he wasn't interrupting anything.

"Hey." Mark's voice sounded warm enough.

Can't have been anything too harsh from the chief.

"Hey. I was wondering if Forsythe and Summers might have shared a prison cell at some point."

"Great minds, *mahasani,*" Mark said. "And guess what? You're right. Not cells exactly, but they were both in Centinela at the same time, three years ago. I put a call in to the warden and he remembered Summers. He did some checking, and when he called me back, he told me both Summers and Forsythe had to be disciplined for getting into a fight over another prisoner…a Ronnie Charleston. I researched Charleston and he's been out for a couple of years. No arrests since and he works at an auto repair shop, EZee Fix, in Compton. I'm going down there to talk to him this afternoon."

"Oh yeah? Be careful, please."

"Aren't I always? Charleston doesn't sound like too much of a threat. Besides, I'll have Deedee with me." He chuckled. "She'll keep me safe."

John smiled. Deedee, or Detective Diana Dixon, had become a friend of theirs in the five years she'd been part of Mark's team. A sassy but able African American raised in Watts, she'd learned the hard way to be tough. She and her wife Jasmine had recently adopted a baby girl and had asked John and Mark to be godfathers.

"Give her a hug from me."

After they'd disconnected the call, John was ill at ease. Too much coffee? No lunch? Was that what the knot in his stomach was all about? Or was it one of those damn funny feelings he got when something seemed off? Mark going to talk to this Ronnie Charleston character…why would that put him on edge? Mark had interviewed hundreds of people over the years, some not very nice people… and Ronnie Charleston hadn't been in trouble since getting out of jail…and Mark was going to have Deedee with him, so why this uneasy feeling?

Shit… If he called Mark, what could he say? *Don't go?* That would sound stupid. Mark was aware of John's fine-tuned instincts, but even John felt he was over-reacting. It was broad daylight, an auto repair shop and he had Deedee with him. What could possibly go wrong?

He grabbed his phone and turned on the GPS. *Time to Compton approximately twenty-seven minutes by car.* On his bike he could shave at least five minutes off that. He'd be there roughly at the same time as Mark and Deedee. If everything looked okay, he'd stay out of sight. *Mark won't even know I was there, and hopefully won't have to…*

"Hey, Millie, I'm gonna take off for a couple of hours, so why don't you go on home early?"

She gave him a shrewd look. "Not getting yourself into any trouble, are you?"

"Of course not…no, no trouble. Just something I have to take care of."

"Hmm. All right. Whatever it is, be careful."

"Aren't I always?" *Shit, now I'm sounding like Mark.*

* * * *

Traffic was light on the freeway and he made it into Compton in good time, hopefully around the same time as Mark and Deedee. EZee Fix was at the corner of the main drag and Halston—*and also EZee to find.* He rolled his eyes at his own joke then drove his bike around to the side of the shop. Mark's car was parked out front and they had obviously already gone inside. He was just about to dismount when a red-haired guy came barreling out of the repair shop heading straight for him, Mark and Deedee in hot pursuit.

What the–? He swung his bike in front of the runaway, who barged into him with enough force to topple him and the bike over. He sprawled onto his side, the redhead on top of him. *Ouch…* The weight on his left leg was suddenly gone and he looked up to see Mark and Deedee holding, none too gently, the redhead's arms.

"Are you all right, sir?" Deedee asked.

"It's John," Mark said with a sigh.

"Oh…" Deedee stared at him through wide eyes. "I didn't recognize you with your visor closed."

"What are you doing here, John?" Mark didn't look happy.

John struggled to his feet. "From the looks of things, stopping this guy from getting away."

"We'd have taken care of that. Okay…" Mark snapped a pair of cuffs on the redhead's wrists. "Mr. Charleston, I'm taking you to the precinct for further questioning. This attempt to run was not a good idea."

"I'd have gotten away," Charleston snarled, "if it hadn't been for this ass." He glared at John and kicked his bike.

"Hey, don't kick a bike when it's down."

Deedee giggled as John bent to drag his bike into an upright position. "So, Detective, you don't have to thank me for my help."

"I wasn't going to. You shouldn't be here. Detective Dixon and I had the situation under control."

Charleston snorted. "Yeah, like hell you did. And one more time…I don't know any David Summers or…or, the other one."

"Let's go." Mark pushed the redhead toward his car.

"See you later then." *I guess no good deed goes unpunished.* But Mark was right. He and Deedee had it under control. So why had he felt the need to come here…and why were his spidey senses along with his stomach still telling him something was wrong? Mark's car pulled out of the lot. Sighing, John was about to follow when two men exited the repair shop. They stopped in their tracks when they spotted John.

How in hell did Mark and Deedee not see these guys…these really big *guys?*

"Help you?" one of them, a real bruiser, barked.

"Uh, is Ronnie around?"

"There's no Ronnie here."

"But he works here, right?"

The bruiser took a step toward John. "I said, there's no Ronnie here."

"That's weird, he told me he worked at the EZee Fix auto repair shop."

"Who the fuck are you?" the other guy, nearly as big as his buddy, plus even meaner-looking, asked.

"I'm John, a friend of Ronnie's. I just came by to see if he wanted to have lunch."

The two guys traded glances with each other. "Well, ya missed him, so take off."

"Oh, so now I missed him," John said with an exaggerated shrug. "But before you said there was no Ronnie here…you know, like he didn't work here, or exist even."

"The fuck are you talkin' about?" The bruiser narrowed his eyes and glared at John. "Get outta here, now."

"Yeah, but now I'm confused. Does Ronnie work here even if you said he didn't? If that's the case, who are you guys? Do you work here? Oh, wait…" John pretended to remember something. "Was that Ronnie I saw being taken away by some guy and a woman who really looked like cops? What did he do? Are you guys in on it too, whatever it is?"

John knew he was treading on dangerous ground. Any minute now and these guys were going to get nasty. Even as he thought it, they lumbered toward him, the bruiser actually growling. John rolled his bike away from them then dismounted. The big guy rushed him first and John, using a defensive move Mark had taught him and one he practiced every chance he got, planted a karate kick into the middle of the guy's chest.

With a surprised "Oof," the bruiser went down, sprawling on his back, his friend almost tripping over him as he advanced on John. He looked down in surprise at his friend on the ground, who appeared to be in no hurry to get up. John knew that kick hurt. He'd been on the receiving end of it a time or two.

"Fucker." The bruiser's friend aimed a punch at John's jaw. John jerked his head back and the punch slid past John's chin. He danced back, the mean-eyed guy barging in, aiming more punches, all of which John, thanks to Mark's expert training, evaded. "Stand fucking still," the man grunted. John jabbed at the meaty jaw in front of him. It startled the guy, who stepped back, falling over his own feet and landing on top of his friend.

John grabbed his cell from his pocket and punched in Mark's number. "Hey, you better get back here or send backup. There were two more dudes in the shop. I kinda got them on the ground right now, but could really use some help." The big guys were getting to their feet. "Like now!"

"Be there in five," was Mark's terse reply.

Five… Could he hold these dudes off for another five minutes? The two were up on their feet, murderous expressions marring their faces. They separated, coming at John from both sides. Mark had taught him how to deal with this too, but these guys were way bigger than the ones he practiced with in the gym. Other than turning and running, he had no choice but to try to fight them off.

Obviously wary of him now, they didn't try rushing him, edging nearer on each side instead, until one was close enough to reach out and grip the front of John's leather jacket while the other snuck up on him from behind, wrapping him in a bear hug. John snapped his head back, connecting with the man's nose. He yelped with pain and his arms dropped away. The guy with the grip on John's jacket pulled him forward and John went with the motion. He planted his hands on the man's shoulders and jerked his knee up into the man's crotch. A gasping moan escaped his assailant's throat but he didn't release, giving his buddy time to get a hold of John again from behind. An arm around his neck in a chokehold and tightening fast made him see stars.

The weight of both men was proving too much for even his lean, muscled strength. *Shit, this is gonna hurt…* One of them kicked John's feet from under him and he was about to hit the ground when the piercing sound of a siren rent the air and a black-and-white patrol car barreled into the shop's parking lot. The two men pushed John out of the way and made a run for it, but the cops were out of the car and one of them snapped out the warning, "Stop, or we'll shoot!"

They stopped and turned around, the bruiser pointing a finger at John. "He was tryin' to steal parts from the shop. We came out to stop him and he put up a fight. You should arrest him."

"Over here." The cop gestured with his gun. "Why did you run if he's the thief?"

Before they could answer, Mark's car pulled into the lot, and John sighed with relief. He'd no doubt get yelled at later, but to John, right now Mark looked more beautiful than ever. He could swear there was a halo over Mark's head as he strode toward them, or was it just the sun glinting off the EZee Fix sign?

"Thanks for answering my call so quickly," Mark said to the cops before facing John's attackers. "Names."

"You got nothin' on us," the bigger guy yelled. "This guy's a thief!"

"No, he's not." Mark eyed the two through hard eyes. "Where were you when we spoke to Ronnie Charleston? Was his running a ruse to help you leave without being seen? What's your connection with Charleston?"

"No connection, and we're not sayin' anything more."

"Okay." Mark read them their rights then directed the two cops to cuff them. "Take them downtown. I'll be questioning you both further, along with Charleston."

The men cast dirty looks at John as they were led away by the cops. Mark stared at him for a long moment before asking, "You okay?"

John nodded. "Sorry. I know I shouldn't have been here—"

"You know you could've been really hurt, right? Those guys outweighed you by about a hundred pounds combined. They could've beaten the crap out of you, John...sent you to the hospital." He sighed and turned to look at Deedee, who had discreetly drifted off and was standing by the car. When he turned back to

John, he asked, "So what d'you think was going on here?"

"Some kind of meeting with Ronnie and the other two. Could be they were tipped off you and Deedee were coming to talk to Ronnie, or his running was an act to give his buddies a chance to slip into the back room till you'd gone."

"Why'd you stay?"

"Something didn't feel right…you know how I get sometimes. That weird instinct of mine."

Mark squeezed John's arm gently. "Thanks. This might be more of a lead than we first thought."

"You're not mad at me?"

"I was…and maybe after I've gone over it again in my head, I might be again. You have a lot to make up for…later tonight."

John's interest perked up immediately. He grinned. "Try not to be home too late."

Chapter Twelve

John stopped at the local deli to get dinner for Mark and himself. After the pizza the night before, he decided they needed something lighter, so he chose a shrimp salad and some Italian bread. When he got home, he pulled into the garage then reset the alarm when he entered the house. He didn't think there would be another attack now that Sam and Jareem were in FBI custody, but Mark had asked him to be careful, so... He stowed the salad in the fridge then went into the bedroom to strip and shower.

His cell was ringing when he turned off the spray. Grabbing a towel, he hurried into the bedroom and picked up his phone. *Sam.* "Hey there, how's it going?"

"Well, they found us a place in Bellflower. It's okay." Sam chuckled before continuing. "Wallace muttered something about it being sweeter than his place. How are you?"

"Good." He ran the towel over his hair as he replied. "Had a run-in with some would-be tough guys earlier, but Mark came to save me. Just another day in the life of a private detective."

"You sound okay, but are you?"

"Oh, yeah. How's Jareem holding up?"

"He's good. He doesn't like Wallace. Says he's rude and probably immoral."

John snorted. "I don't know about the immoral bit, but have to agree about his being rude. I get the feeling Wallace's mother didn't care for him much, either. Have they said anything about their plans for you?"

"Not so far. Henderson said it'll take a few days before a decision will be made. I did mention my lectures, the first one coming up in Irvine at the end of next week, and he said he'd see what could be done. Doesn't sound too promising, does it? I really hate to cancel and let them down, but I guess we're at the agency's mercy, so to speak."

"Yeah, tricky. They'd be leery of letting you and Jareem out in public in case his father's hired thugs try some kind of attack."

"At least that would flush them out," Sam said bitterly. "If they fail again and some of them get arrested, they might just give up."

"Sam, the agents are not going to allow you to set yourself up as bait for fucking murderers, so don't even broach that subject. Right now, they're investigating who else along with Kyle Brenton, the bad cop, might be involved, or if he was working alone. A background check on him will reveal if he had prior connections with any Muslim group or if he was just in it for the money...which would be my first guess."

There was silence on the other end, so John made a quick change of topic. "They feeding you good?"

"Oh yeah. We have a menu to choose from and there's a good supply of water and soft drinks. No booze, which is okay. Jareem doesn't drink and it won't hurt me to do without for a while."

"Once this is all over," John said, "I'll get you an invitation to my father-in-law's house for a barbecue. He does the best damn steak you'll ever eat. He has a secret blend of herbs and spices to die for, and the nasty old man won't share it with me."

"Does Mark know you call his dad a nasty old man?"

"No..." John laughed. "And he's not. He's actually the sweetest guy. He's taken the place of my biological father."

"That's great. Okay, looks like I have to go." Sam had lowered his voice. "They're changing shifts and we have to meet the new agents. I hope Wallace's replacement is easier to get along with."

"That's almost a guarantee, right?"

Sam chuckled. "You got it. Talk with you later. Please keep in touch with us."

"Will do. Bye." John went back into the bathroom to finish drying his hair then comb it through, leaving it unfastened to fall to the middle of his back. He put on a pair of shorts and a T-shirt, then padded into the kitchen to make some herbal tea. His mother regularly sent him a mix of home-grown herbs. She'd told him on one of his visits home, with an added wink, that it would increase his *vigor*. So far, he'd found no cause to complain.

Sitting at the table sipping his tea, he relived the moments outside the auto repair shop. Mark had been right. He'd been foolish to take on those two bozos by himself. If the cops hadn't arrived at precisely the right time, he'd have had the crap beaten out of him, for sure. Their weight alone would have kept him pinned down while they pounded and kicked him. It wouldn't have been the first time he'd been in a tight spot, but some were easier to get out of than others.

He wondered where David Summers figured in all this. The redhead, Ronnie Charleston, was the guy Summers and Donald Forsythe, Alex's blackmailer, had fought over in prison. Ronnie was somehow involved with the two heavies at the repair shop, and John was reminded of Alex's claim that he'd seen Forsythe talking to two men in the park just before Alex had found him stabbed to death. He knew Mark would be making those same deductions. Maybe he could help him connect the dots.

* * * *

"Hi, babe." Mark sounded okay even if he looked tired when he got home later that night.

They kissed for a long time, with Mark muttering that he should shower each time they came up for air. "Go on then," John finally said. "I got dinner, so I'll get it ready while you clean up. It's salad, so no fuss. Like some white wine?"

"Please. I'll be quick. Got a lot to tell you."

"Figured." John smiled as Mark disappeared into the bedroom. Despite all the shit that got thrown at them from time to time, the best part of the day for John was when they were together alone. Yeah, he enjoyed a night out with their friends, or getting together with Jack and his buddies. But John loved the nights when it was just Mark and him. When they shared a meal, conversation, a glass of wine, then invariably sweet sex that always left him the happiest of men.

When Mark reappeared, he was wearing shorts and a blue T-shirt that accentuated the blue of his eyes. *Gorgeous…* John dragged him into his arms and laid a scorching kiss on his lips. "No way is dinner going to interfere with this," he said huskily, steering Mark back into the bedroom.

What little they were wearing was thrown on the floor before they fell onto the bed, Mark on top of John's writhing body, pinning him down by his wrists. He traced John's chest with slow, deliberate kisses, lingering over John's nipples to lick and suck them into tiny hard peaks. John bucked in response, grinding their erections together, and Mark kissed his way south over John's torso, all the way down to his crotch. He had to release John's wrists as he nuzzled his lips into John's groin, his stubbled cheek grazing the head of John's cock, making his body jolt with expectation.

That expectation was fulfilled when Mark ran his tongue up the length of John's shaft to the head, lingering over the pre-cum that spilled from the slit. "Mmm…delicious as always," he murmured, raising his head to wink at John. "Here, taste…"

He scooted up to let John suck on his tongue. "Turn over," he mumbled into John's mouth.

Without hesitation, John did as ordered—his interrupted dream of the other night was about to come true. Mark licked and kissed his way down John's spine to the cleft between his butt cheeks. John writhed under him when Mark teased the puckered entrance to his opening with the tip of his tongue. John arched his ass into Mark's touch as he palmed each cheek, separating them to give himself greater access to John's hole. John moaned when Mark went deep, his tongue's action bringing a crescendo of moans and whimpers of pleasure from John. Mark pushed his forefinger in alongside his tongue and, using his saliva as lubricant, stroked the sensitive gland inside John's tight passage. A long groan escaped John and he raised his hips to take all of Mark's thick finger inside, wriggling his butt for maximum enjoyment. If he lived to be a hundred, he'd never get tired of this. No matter that he and Mark had made love over and over, each time was almost like a new experience.

He shivered when Mark replaced his finger with a cool gel that quickly warmed under Mark's touch. The blunt head of Mark's cock breached John's opening and John drew in a deep breath, exhaling slowly as Mark pushed past his resistance. He slid all the way in, grazing John's prostate, giving him another jolt of pleasure. John raised himself to his knees, arching his pelvis into Mark's long, solid thrusts.

"Oh, my God, Mark, that is so amazing, so wonderful. I love you, my big man, love you when you fuck me so well, so hard..." More nonsense spilled from his lips as Mark quickened the pace, ramming into John's tight heat.

"Yeah, you love this, don't you?" Mark growled and slapped John's ass on both cheeks.

"Yes, I love it..." He pushed himself up against Mark's chest and turned his head, searching for Mark's kiss. Their lips meshed in a hot, searing kiss that brought a visceral moan from John as they breathed into each other's mouths. John sank down over Mark's cock while Mark thrust upward, driving himself even deeper inside John, who groaned out his ecstasy against Mark's lips. Mark suddenly pulled out, making John yelp.

"It's okay, *mahasani,*" Mark murmured. "I've got you." He maneuvered John onto his back. Now on top, Mark pushed inside John again and increased the rhythm between them to an almost fever-pitch. John wrapped his arms and legs around Mark's torso, clinging to him, holding fast as they rode the waves of ecstasy together.

"Gonna come…" John pulled Mark down and fastened his lips over Mark's, breathing him in, claiming him, body and soul. Mark gripped John's rock-hard erection, pumping it to match the rhythm of their bodies while he drove deeper inside John. John groaned and he stiffened under Mark as he gave in to the wrenching orgasm he couldn't hold back a moment longer.

"Mark!" He clenched his ass muscles around the base of Mark's cock, urging him on to his own climax, wanting to shout with joy when the hot surge of Mark's release filled him completely. They collapsed onto their sides, Mark still deep inside John, who sighed happily as blissful euphoria enveloped him.

He must have dozed off because when he came to, Mark was still there, but he must have cleaned them up as there was no stickiness between them. "Did you wash me?" he murmured, his lips on Mark's.

"Yes, you were gross."

"Was not!" He slapped Mark's bare chest lightly. "Take that back."

"Okay, but while I have you here, all limp and unable to get away from me, I'm gonna say this. You were very brave today, but also foolhardy. I shudder to think what might have happened if I hadn't got those officers there in time. Please do not put yourself in that kind of position again." He put his fingers on John's lips when he started to interrupt. "Let me finish. I know you can handle yourself well, and your martial arts skills are most likely better than some of my officers, but two against one, especially two guys who looked like they could take on the Hulk and win…not clever, John. Next time, back off, jump on your bike and get the hell out of there. Okay?"

When John started to protest, Mark tapped him on the nose. "I'm only saying this because I love you and would hate like hell to see you beaten so badly you'd have to be hospitalized. Those guys, once they got you on the ground, would've kicked the shit outta you. So, please, err on the side of caution in future." He kissed John and tightened his arms around him.

"Okay, Daddy."

"Don't get cute. Just promise you'll do as I ask."

"I promise."

"Good boy. Now get up and fix my dinner."

* * * *

"So, how'd it go with the terrible threesome?" John asked while he poured them both a glass of Chardonnay. "Did they cave real fast?"

"Nope. They said they didn't know anything about any dead guy, didn't know a David Summers or an Alex Vasquez. Didn't know about any blackmailing scheme. All they did, they told me, was mind their own business and lead quiet lives."

John almost choked on the wine he'd started to sip. "And you believed them, of course."

"Right. So I had them separated and questioned them one by one. Ronnie was the first to give it up. Yes, he knew Summers and he'd met Alex. He even admitted to a three-way with them, but he didn't know where Summers was, nor did he know Alex had been murdered. He looked and sounded sufficiently shocked when I told him about Alex that I believed him."

"But what about his association with the other two?"

"He said he didn't know them till they showed up today at the repair shop. This is the part of his story I don't believe. He said they wanted to know where Summers was. Apparently, they're involved with Summers in some kind of a deal they did for him. Ronnie told them he hadn't seen Summers in days. They were about to beat the crap out of him when Deedee and I showed up. They told him to run as soon as we came in the shop to give them time to get away. Meantime, they slid into the back room, so Ronnie took off just as they ordered him to. He said he felt safer with us cops than with the other two."

"Smart kid. Wonder if he'd have kept going if he hadn't run into me?"

"We'd have caught him eventually." Mark chuckled. "That cyclone fence around the property would've stopped him in his tracks."

"So, the other two?"

"Ah, yeah. Different story. Sid Renner and Chaz Martin. Records as long as your arm. Assault, drug use and pushing, armed robbery. Renner even had a rape charge, but the woman backed off when it came to court. Said she couldn't quite remember if it was him even though she'd identified him earlier in a line-up."

"Maybe she was scared."

"I think you're right. So, with all that on their records, it's not too much of a stretch to believe they could've killed Alex, and probably his blackmailer too. I'm holding them pending further investigation. And that's where you come in." Mark leaned in and kissed John lightly on the lips.

"On the quiet, naturally. I'm going to release Ronnie tomorrow. I have a feeling he'll lead us straight to Summers. I'll have detectives working on it too, of course, but I'd like you in the background, so to speak. See what you can find out, but remember what you promised. Do not get in a confrontation with either of them. Understood?"

"Aye, aye, Skipper."

Mark sighed. "We have seventy-two hours before I have to charge them or let them go."

John smirked. "No pressure then."

"Glad you see it that way."

Chapter Thirteen

Mark had told John he was releasing Ronnie Charleston in the morning, most likely after ten, so John figured waiting for him outside the precinct then tailing him could put him on the fast track to see who he would contact first. Around ten thirty, Ronnie ran down the steps, cell phone in hand. John watched him punch a number into his cell then, after a brief conversation, he paced around outside the building. Obviously, someone was coming to pick him up. Would it be Summers…or maybe Ronnie's mom?

After about twenty minutes, a red Mustang convertible pulled up and Ronnie climbed in. Summers' mugshot had shown him at his worst, looking as if he'd just come off a mighty big bender, his clothes disheveled, his eyes glazed and distant. The young man driving the Mustang and wearing a pink polo shirt was fairly handsome, his hair styled, if a little windblown from having the top down. *You clean up well,* was John's thought as he slipped around the corner where he'd parked his bike.

He waited until the Mustang took off then rolled out onto the street two cars behind it. Summers took the 110 Freeway to the 101, getting off on Santa Monica Boulevard. The car separating John from Summers' Mustang veered off, showing John that Ronnie had his arm around Summers' shoulder and was kissing his face.

So, more than just friends… Looks like Ronnie appreciated being fought over in jail. He slowed and let another car get in between him and the Mustang. Just before La Cienega, Summers turned right onto a narrow, hilly street lined on both sides by apartment blocks. The Mustang disappeared into an off-street parking garage. John rode by then pulled over and called Mark.

"Hi," he said when Mark picked up. "I'm in West Hollywood. Summers has an apartment at eight-twenty West Elm Street. He and Ronnie Charleston just went in. Don't know the apartment number yet."

"Okay, good work, John. I'll send two detectives over there to charge Summers with trying to evade arrest."

"I can do some more snooping." He dismounted and walked down the hilly street to the front of the apartment block. "Looks like there's only six or eight apartments. Shouldn't take much to see which one they're in."

"No, let the detectives do that. You can back off now."

"But—"

"John…I said, back off."

"Oh, okay. I could say my work here is done, but it's only half done really, Officer."

"John," Mark growled.

"Yeah, yeah, I'm going, sir."

"Good boy. See you later."

Peeved, John walked up the hill to where he'd left his bike. He drove farther up the hill, then turned and found a good vantage point to survey the building. Even though Mark hadn't asked him to wait until the cops got there, he decided it might be a good idea in case whatever Summers and Charleston were doing didn't take them long and they left. He could at least tail them and give Mark a heads-up about their location.

It took the cops close to twenty minutes to show up... *And wouldn't you know it? Those guys are leaving! Must have been a real quick fuck...maybe just a blow job.* The detectives' car was unmarked, but something must have alerted Summers to the fact that they were cops, because he grabbed Ronnie's arm and started to run.

The detectives yelled for them to stop, but the two men ignored the order. John recognized the detectives from his visits to Mark's office. Bill Watts and his partner, Terry Parker, gave chase. John gunned his bike and zoomed across the street in an effort to intercept them. Summers hit John's front wheel with his knees and crashed to the ground, while Ronnie, after a moment's hesitation, skirted John's bike and took off up the hill.

Bill Watts, tall and built, hauled Summers to his feet and clapped handcuffs on him, while Terry started running after the redhead.

"Hop on," John told him. "Better chance of catching him." Terry sprang onto the pillion and John took off. Ronnie was a sprinter and had reached the top of the hill faster than John had expected. There was a roadworks sign up ahead and Ronnie was leaping over trenches and concrete pipes in a desperate attempt to shake off John and the detective.

John stared ahead to where the roadworks ended. A high wall was going to prevent Ronnie from going anywhere but back onto the road. As if realizing this, Ronnie launched himself at the wall, missing the top of it by a few inches. He slithered down the stone frontage, landing in one of the trenches. John halted his bike, letting Terry leap off the pillion and head for the spot where Ronnie had disappeared into the trench.

Moments later, Terry climbed out, pushing a handcuffed and downcast Ronnie in front of him. "Thanks for your help, John." A black car pulled up behind them and Bill got out, grinning at them.

"Got your exercise for the day, Terry." He clapped a big hand on John's shoulder. "We'll let the sarge know you were on the ball with the bike."

"Uh, maybe downplay that some," John said warily. "He kinda told me to stand down when you guys arrived, if you catch my drift…"

Bill and Terry chuckled while Ronnie snarled, "Fucker," and kicked the front wheel of John's bike. "You guys have nothin' on me, anyways. I'll sue for harassment and false arrest."

"Running from officers of the law and consorting with persons under investigation as suspects in a murder case is hardly nothing," Terry told him. "You better get yourself a good attorney."

Ronnie's face went almost as red as his hair. "I had nothin'. to do with any murder. Dave promised he'd take care of it."

"Dave, being David Summers?" John asked.

Ronnie nodded sullenly. From inside the car, a voice yelled, "Shut your stupid fucking mouth!"

Terry's lips twisted in a wry smile. "Let's go. You can do all your explaining at the precinct. Thanks again, John."

"Be seeing you around," Bill said as he led Ronnie, who never stopped insisting he'd done nothing wrong, to the car.

John watched as Ronnie was shoved into the back of the car alongside Summers. *Hope you had fun earlier, 'cause I wouldn't want to be ya right now, Ronnie. Man, if looks could kill, you'd be one dead redhead.*

* * * *

When he got home, John called Sam to check in with him. He sounded in good spirits, telling John that the FBI had okayed his upcoming lectures.

"They're sending whichever agent is available with me," he told John. "But Jareem has to stay put, which is a bummer, although we understand it'd be risky for them to keep eyes on both of us. He'll be okay here with another of the agents."

"How's Wallace treating you?"

"I've decided he's a very unhappy man," Sam remarked. "It's obvious he doesn't like his job, which honestly I can't say I blame him for. Playing watchdog over two male adults is not, I think, why he joined the FBI. I've heard Henderson have some sharp words with him, but his disposition hasn't improved. I did mention it to Henderson yesterday, suggesting perhaps he ask for a new posting, but he said Wallace just has to grin and bear it for now."

"Which he's really not into, right?"

"No, he considers this a waste of his time and training."

"Oh, sorry, Sam. Mark's on the other line. I better take his call. Talk to you later."

"No problem. Later."

"Hey, Mark. How's it going?"

"Well, they all lawyered up, so it's all on hold until tomorrow, when I meet with them and the lawyers. I'm having the deputy DA sit in on it. I'm more and more convinced that Summers hired Renner and Martin to kill Donald Forsythe, Alex's blackmailer. As much as they pretend they don't know one another, I can tell by the body language, and the looks they think I don't notice, that they're lying. Renner and Martin don't like Summers. And there's something about Renner that worries me."

"You mean, apart from the fact that he's a convicted felon?"

Mark chuckled. "Yeah, there is that. But something about his demeanor is what I mean. His eyes never stop moving, like darting all over the room, sideways, up and down, and his right leg jiggles constantly. He's either a nervous wreck or he's missing his meds."

"What's left of a bad drug habit, maybe?"

"Could be."

"What about Ronnie?"

"He's their weakest link. He's scared. The only thing that stops him from coming clean is that he's infatuated with Summers. But, from the way Summers was reacting, I don't think he returns the feeling. I almost feel sorry for the kid."

"Huh. I thought they'd gone over to Summers' apartment for some nookie," John said, "but maybe not. They were in and out kinda quick."

"Well, Ronnie asked him if his lawyer could help him and Summers told him to get his own, that he wasn't in the habit of paying other people's attorney fees. So the kid is left with a court-appointed lawyer, along with the two heavies. Like I said, Summers is not Mr. Popularity. I am so tempted to put them all in the same cell and see who comes out with the most bruises."

John laughed. "You wouldn't do that, would you?"

"Naw, it's against procedure anyway, but my evil mind enjoyed the thought of what might happen." Mark chuckled. "Anyway, I'm almost through here till tomorrow morning. Wanna go for an early dinner?"

"Name the time and place, I'll be there."

* * * *

Halfway through their dinner at Danilo's Mediterranean Restaurant, Mark got a call from Stan, the coroner.

"Hate to interrupt anything important, but I thought you should know this."

Mark pushed his plate away. "Go ahead, Stan."

"The knife that killed Donald Forsythe is, as I thought at the time, an antique, and most likely should not have been left in the body. It's quite rare and worth several thousands of dollars. Brett tracked it down to an antique store in Westwood. The dealer had reported a break-in at his store and the knife is listed as one of the items stolen."

"Okay, good work, Stan. Tell Brett thanks, too. You have the name and phone number of the store owner?"

"I do."

"Email me the info and a picture of the knife. If he's still in his shop, I'll go over there now. Thanks, Stan."

He hung up and asked John, "Fancy a trip to Westwood?"

"You bet."

Mark's cell chimed with the information Stan had sent him. He quickly punched in the phone number. "Robert Langston? Oh, hi, this is Detective Sergeant Mark Rossi with the LAPD. You reported a break-in about a month ago. I'm following up on that. We may have located one of the items listed as stolen. A knife with a carved ivory handle."

John could hear the owner's excited exclamation.

"I'd like to come talk to you if you're available tonight. Good." Mark nodded. "About a half hour or so depending on the traffic. Right. Thank you, Mr. Langston. I'll see you soon." Mark paid the bill and they headed out to the parking lot. "We'll take my car, John. Your bike'll be okay under that light."

"Yeah, and the alarm's on, so we're good."

On the way, Mark said, "With both Renner and Martin's record of robbery, could it be that the antique knife ended up in their possession?"

"But why leave it behind in Forsythe's body?" John asked.

"They may not have realized just how valuable it was, or they were in too much of a hurry to get away before Alex showed up. Stan said there no prints on the handle, so they probably thought it couldn't be traced to them."

"Little did they know about our Stan and Brett the tenacious."

Mark grinned. "Right, but of course, we still have to prove they're the thieves."

"Maybe a quick visit to scope out their home…homes. Do they live together?"

Mark handed him his phone. "Can't remember, but I got 'em listed in there. Take a look."

John thumbed through the directory list. "Chaz Martin lives at forty-two thirty-four Front Street, space twenty-two, in Compton, and Sid Renner is at…bingo—same address." He frowned. "Please tell me they're not gay lovers."

"Don't think so." Mark chuckled. "They shared a cell for a couple of years, so it's most likely a marriage of convenience."

John shuddered. "The thought of those two doing it makes me want to gag. Anyway, while they're in the pokey, couldn't we take a look inside their place?"

"We could, but anything we'd find would be inadmissible without a warrant."

"Okay," John persisted, "but what if we find something, leave it where it is and you get a warrant in the morning then go back and get whatever it is we find? Presuming we find stuff, of course."

"Devious, but it might be worth a shot. I could talk with Judge Eunice Harper. She…uh…she kinda likes me."

"Of course she does. Everybody likes you, Mark." John glanced slyly at him. "How much does she like you?"

"I don't know…but she sorta flirts when we bump into each other."

"It's those blue eyes of yours. And your studly body, and your lips, and— Should I be jealous?"

"Only if I was straight and into the motherly type. She has to be in her sixties."

"And there's no way you're straight," John said, laughing. "No straight guy kisses another guy the way you kiss me, making me hard in seconds. I don't think you could've fooled me about that for the last ten years."

Mark smiled. "There is that."

"So, you'll get the warrant?"

"Yeah, and if I get in trouble, I can always blame you."

* * * *

Langston's Antiques had a small frontage, but the space inside went a long way back. The high walls were covered with an eclectic collection of paintings, shields, embroidered rugs and Native American blankets. Both sides of the aisle featured glass cabinets filled with glittering jewelry of all sizes and stones.

"Hope he's insured for a lot of money," Mark muttered.

John grinned. "So many beautiful things…which one shall I buy?"

"Ah!" A tall silver-haired man walked toward them, a beaming smile on his face. "A quote from the musical, *Kismet*." His carefully enunciated words told them he was British. "Not one I'd expect to hear from a policeman. I'm Robert Langston, the owner of this establishment."

"Maybe from a private detective? Hi, I'm John White Eagle." He held out his hand. "This is Detective Sergeant Mark Rossi."

"A pleasure to meet you both." Langston beamed at John. "White Eagle, eh? Cheyenne?"

"Dakota Sioux."

"Ah, I do believe I have some artwork from that tribe."

"You sure have a lot of stuff, here, Mr. Langston," Mark said, looking around. "Hate to be you on inventory night."

Langston laughed. "I usually cajole a friend or two to help out. I ply them with food and wine to make it more fun." He smiled then added, "But, of course, you're here for more serious business."

"Right." Mark pulled his phone from his jacket's inside pocket and scrolled to the information Stan had sent him. He turned the screen toward Langston. "Is this the knife that was stolen?"

'"Is this a dagger which I see before me?'" Langston intoned with a wry smile. "No doubt you know that one too, Mr. White Eagle?"

John nodded. "Macbeth's vision of his future."

"It is indeed. Good to know that our tax dollars for education aren't going completely to waste. And yes, Detective Sergeant Rossi," Langston continued, either ignoring or unaware of John's eye roll, "this is the knife in question. Made in India circa fourteen hundred and twenty-five. Hand-carved of course, made of the finest ivory, and valued at twenty-five thousand dollars. You said you think you have located it?"

"Yes. I'm afraid we can't return it to you just yet," Mark told him. "It's evidence in a murder investigation."

Langston stared at him wide-eyed. "Good gracious."

"Do you have a list of any other items that were stolen?" Mark asked.

"Yes, yes. I'll get it for you." He hurried off, returning a few moments later with the list printed on a sheet of paper. "I thought you might ask, so I made a copy for you."

"Thanks." Mark took the paper from Langston, scanned it briefly then folded it and slipped it into his inside pocket. "Well, thank you, Mr. Langston. We'll be in touch with regard to the other missing items and, once we've found the culprits, we'll get your *dagger* back to you."

"I wish you well, then, and a quick end to your investigation. A murder, indeed… Goodness, who'd have thought?" Langston paused, then said, "If it's of any help at all, whoever stole the items will not find them easy to unload. Some of the jewelry is priceless and certainly no pawn shop owner worth his salt would touch most of it. They couldn't come anywhere near the value, and collectors would be very wary indeed of purchasing from an unknown vendor."

They exited the store and made for Mark's car. John nudged Mark with his elbow. "So tell me, sir, how do you feel about your tax dollars going to good use so I can quote lines from musicals and Shakespearean plays?"

Mark chuckled. "I thought that might get a rise outta you."

"Not really. I got used to it a long time ago. Some people are still surprised when they find out we *Injuns* actually went to college. Anyway, I have a feeling that the dagger in question might have been used in a murder before," John said. "Most likely sacrificial. It looks lethal enough."

"From its history, it very well could've been." Mark unlocked his car. "Okay, let's go do some illegal snooping."

Chapter Fourteen

John knew that it was stereotypical of him to not be surprised by the seedy state of the Renner and Martin home. It was little more than a trailer in a rundown RV park close to the railroad tracks. There being no security gate and no well-lit roads to scare off would-be vandals made it easy for John and Mark to park alongside the ramshackle dwelling, and for Mark to pick the lock in seconds.

"Good thing you're on the right side of the law," John whispered as the door squeaked open.

Mark grunted. "Doesn't feel like I am right now."

Inside was a shambles, and John couldn't imagine how two men as big as Renner and Martin could cope in the tiny space.

"Maybe they don't spend too much time here," John remarked, looking around with disgust.

"Would you?"

John chuckled. "Only if you promised me the world and all its gold tomorrow."

"Okay, let's get moving here." Mark pulled the list from his pocket. "Two gold and diamond bracelets, three gold stopwatches, five diamond necklaces, a tiara…a *tiara*? A gold coin collection worth, get this, two hundred thousand dollars…"

"There's a carry-on bag here on the lower bunk," John said. "I'm almost afraid to unzip it in case something furry jumps out."

"Unzip it anyway. If they're going to have a hard time unloading the merchandise, like Langston said, it might all still be here."

John unzipped the bag. Nothing jumped out, but he recoiled anyway as the reek of unwashed clothes hit his nostrils. "Ughew!" He closed the bag quickly, his face screwed up in disgust.

Mark laughed. "What was that sound you made?"

"Oh my God, these guys are pigs."

"They're not followers of Martha Stewart, that's for sure." Mark stared at the bed with disgust. "Look at those sheets. They haven't been washed in weeks, judging by the state of them."

"Let's keep searching and get outta here fast as we can before we catch their cooties."

"Okay, so look under the bed while I check the closet."

"Oh, great," John muttered, wincing as he knelt on the dirty rug. Trouble was, the bunk bed was so low, John had to stretch his body out on the floor so he could peer under it. He winced as the side of his face brushed against the smelly carpet pile. *And to think this was my idea…* Tentatively, he reached under the bed, groping around, but came back with nothing more than a collection of dust bunnies and streaks of some unknown substance on his bare arm. *God…*

"Find anything?" Mark was still rummaging in the closet.

"Nothing I want to talk about."

Mark glanced at him over his shoulder. "You're not getting in my car with that dirty arm. Go wash it off in the bathroom. Just put everything back where it belongs."

Grumbling, John stepped inside the tiny bathroom. He didn't want to touch anything, but had to turn on the faucet, which he did using only his fingertips. He used toilet paper to dry off. No way was he putting the filthy towel anywhere near his skin. He was just about to turn and scoot as quick as he could out of the bathroom when he spotted a barely visible short string hanging from the side of the toilet tank.

"Huh." He lifted the lid and yelped with delight. "Mark, look what I just found." He pulled a plastic bag out of the water, the glittering contents catching what little light there was in the room.

"What? Wow… Well done, John." Mark gave him a smacking kiss on the cheek. They both stared at the contents of the bag. Gold bracelets, diamond necklaces, and yes, even the tiara was there. "Fantastic. Okay, put it back the way you found it. I'll get that warrant in the morning and have Bill come out with me to search the premises. A little underhanded, but hey, those guys belong in the slammer."

John dropped the bag back into the tank and replaced the lid. "And I belong in the shower. Can't wait to get out of these clothes."

"When have I heard that before?" Mark snickered. "Oh yeah, last night and the night before…and the night—"

"Save it." John grabbed Mark's arm and hustled him out of the trailer. "You're the one who'll benefit from it all, so pedal to the metal, man of mine, and let's go home."

* * * *

First thing in the morning, Mark drove over to the courthouse and scanned the list of judges on duty. He grinned when he saw Judge Harper's name there. He had a chance at a warrant without too much trouble from her…maybe. Eunice was no pushover, but he was aware that she did like him better than some of the other official men and women she had to deal with.

He knocked on her door then ducked his head inside. "Good morning, Judge Harper, Can I have a moment of your time?"

"Sure thing, Mark. Come on in and take a seat. What are you up to this morning?"

He sat, giving the older woman, who was already wearing her robes, the smile that John said melted people's bones. "No good, as usual. How are you?"

"Always good, Mark. What else must a judge be?" They chuckled together. "So what can I do for you?"

He quickly recounted the case he was investigating. "The interesting thing is that the knife that was used to kill Forsythe is an antique, and worth several thousands of dollars."

"And it was left *in situ*?"

"Yes. They either didn't realize its value or they were in a hurry to get away. Our coroner researched the knife and found that it had been stolen from an antique store along with several other items. I spoke with the store owner and he gave me a list of the other stolen goods. I'd like a warrant to search the home of the two suspects. If the swag is there, I can press charges."

Judge Harper nodded. "Seems likely that some of it at least might be there."

"Or all. The store owner said it'd be rough getting rid of it. Some of it is priceless, and not too many pawn shops are up for that kind of expensive deal, especially if they don't know who's trying to pawn the items."

"You have the suspects?"

"Yes, I'm holding them while we investigate a murder case that I'm pretty sure they're involved in. But I'll have to let them go if I don't have anything to prove my suspicions that they killed Forsythe, the blackmailer. A friend of John's was also murdered and is tied to the case."

"Sounds as if you have your hands full. Okay, I'll draw up a warrant." Harper smiled as she pulled a document from her desk filing cabinet. "How is John?"

"He's good. He was involved with an international case, but the FBI have it now, so he should be either at home, or at his office, relaxing."

"Unlikely, knowing him."

Mark sighed. "I'm afraid you might be right."

* * * *

John, seated at his desk, stared at the man sitting across from him and tried hard to hide his dislike. "Mr. Dunlop, are you feeling okay? You're swaying in your seat."

"I might've had one too many at lunch." Dunlop dug his chin into his chest and hiccupped. "Anyway, my wife's who I wanna talk about, not me. She's cheating on me and I want you to find out who the fuck it is, so I can punch his fucking lights out."

John was glad Millie was still out on her break. Now that Sam and Jareem's case was out of his hands, he needed some new clients to help pay the rent on his office. But this guy was not someone he'd enjoy working for. He was the type that wanted a quick resolution so it didn't end up costing him more than he thought it should. He'd be a pain in the ass, calling every five minutes demanding John do his job more efficiently.

"Okay, Mr. Dunlop, give me the details and I'll check it out for you. I can't, however, put anyone in danger. When I find the man involved, you can't go punching his lights out, as you put it. That could result in injury, and your arrest. Don't think that would solve the problems you and your wife are having. Okay?"

"Just find him," Dunlop growled. "After that, it's none of your business what I do about it."

"I'm afraid that's not true. My involvement with you if you injure this person could result in me losing my license. Sorry, but unless you guarantee that you will not harm the man, I cannot work for you. Simple as that."

Dunlop stared at John, his jaw working but no words coming out. Finally, he lurched off the seat. "Fuck you!" He stormed out of John's office. John sighed. No way could he work for a man like that. He'd no doubt find another private detective to help him… *And good luck to him, whoever he is.*

The outer door opened and Millie hurried in, her face flushed. "Please tell me you did not take that horribly rude man on as a client."

"I didn't. Why, what did he do?"

"Almost pushed me down the stairs. I gave him a piece of my mind and he gave me the finger."

"That ass."

"Don't worry, I gave him the finger back."

John laughed out loud. "I'd liked to have seen that! His wife's cheating on him, if you can believe it."

"I can believe it, and I wouldn't blame her. Why any woman would marry a cretin like that is beyond me." She sat at her desk as the office phone rang. "JWE Investigations, how may I direct your call?" she asked sweetly, her anger gone. "Oh, hello, Mark. How are you? I am well, thank you. John is standing right here. You sound as if you have something important to tell him, so I'll connect you right away. Have a lovely day, bye." She patched the call through to John's cell.

"How's it goin', *mahasani*?"

"I have the mother of all headaches from listening to Renner and Martin yelling at Summers. They're blaming him for everything while he just sits there and lets his lawyer, Brett Silver, do the talking. Silver's good. He counters every single thing the heavies are throwing at Summers, but there's no doubt in my mind that Summers is guilty of having Forsythe killed.

"I think when this goes to court, Renner and Martin will cave. They almost shit themselves when I laid that bag of gold and diamonds on the table, along with the search warrant. I thought Renner was gonna have a seizure, like he knew he was sunk and jail time was unavoidable. Frank Lovett, the deputy DA, wants to bring in Art Klein for the prosecution."

"The big guns, huh?"

"Art is excellent at getting to the truth. Anyway, they're remanded until tomorrow, when they'll get to plead before a judge. Frank's going for no bail on account of them being a flight risk."

"Can you charge them with Alex's murder also?" John asked.

"Soon as I get something from forensics. I'm hoping for prints or DNA in the car other than Alex's."

"What about Ronnie?" John asked.

"Frank and I questioned him on his own. He had a court-appointed attorney, young and eager, who kept telling Ronnie he didn't have to answer our questions. Frank charged him with resisting arrest, twice, and consorting with suspects in a murder case. So—"

Anything else Mark was about to say was stopped short by the sound of gun shots.

"Jesus...John, I have to go!"

"Mark! What the hell?"

"What's wrong, John?" Millie wanted to know.

"Something happened at the precinct. Shots fired. Shit, I have to get over there."

Millie grabbed his arm. "No, you don't, John. You'd never get near the place if there's a shooting. They'll have the area cordoned off. Sit tight and wait for Mark to call again."

"But—" John sat heavily back in his chair.

"You know I'm right." Millie patted his arm. "You know you'd just be adding to the confusion trying to get through to make sure Mark is all right. I'll turn on the TV. Something like this is bound to have the media's attention."

* * * *

Mark unholstered his Berretta and stepped out of his office. The other detectives in the bullpen were likewise arming themselves.

"Anyone know what happened?" Mark yelled over the excited clamor.

"No, sarge," one of them said loudly.

Mark pulled open the door into the hallway that led to the interrogation rooms and cells. "Shit almighty..." Renner was surrounded by officers and holding them at bay with what looked like a police issue handgun. Summers lay prone on the floor, blood seeping from under him. *Fuck...* Mark stepped through the line of officers to confront Renner.

"Renner..." Mark kept his voice low and even as he faced the big man. "Don't make things worse for yourself. Put the gun down and let's talk this over."

Renner stared at him, fury in his eyes. "That rat bastard was throwing us under the bus. He had his fancy lawyer do all the talking." He aimed the gun at Brett Silver, who cringed against the wall. "But he knows as well as me and Martin that Summers organized everything. He hired us to off Forsythe, then his boyfriend when Vasquez got cold feet and wanted to go see you guys."

"Okay, but what are you doing now?" Mark holstered his gun in an attempt to appear less threatening. He took a step nearer Renner. "You know you can't leave here. There are too many of us and only one of you. You won't make it to the exit. So put the gun down and—"

"And face a fucking lifetime in prison? Not happening. That fuck deserved to die, but I can't face another jail sentence, so..." He put the gun under his chin, closed his eyes and pulled the trigger. There was a resounding click as the hammer hit an empty chamber. For a moment everyone, including Renner, froze. Then, as one, the officers piled on top of Renner, took the gun from him and cuffed him. He stood, shoulders drooped, looking as though he might burst into tears.

"How did he manage to get that gun?" Mark demanded. "Why weren't they cuffed?"

"We were in the process of cuffing them, to take them back to the cells," one of the officers replied. "He grabbed Smithy's gun so fast, then pulled Summers out here and shot him. It happened so damn quick—"

"All right. Get them back to the cells and call a medic." He knelt by Summers and felt for a pulse. None. The man was dead. "Get the coroner up here too."

Mark stood and sighed. *What a mess…* The media would be all over this one. Man shot while in custody using one of the police officers' guns. *Great. They'll accuse us of being slipshod, careless, uncaring about prisoners' safety. All the usual stuff.* He groaned when Chief Oates rounded the corner and came straight toward him looking very unhappy.

Not getting out of here any time soon tonight…

Chapter Fifteen

One week later

John had talked with Sam almost every day since he and Jareem had been holed up in the safe house. They'd developed an easygoing over-the-phone relationship, but this time, the news Sam had for him was surprising and potentially worrying.

"Jareem's brother, Feisal, arrived in LA yesterday. He's arranged a meeting with Jareem for later this afternoon at three. Not here. Henderson said it would compromise the security of the safe house if the brother knew the location. Permission has been given as long as there are agents in attendance."

"No need to ask why he's here, I guess."

"If you're guessing it's to talk Jareem into going back home with him, you'd be right,' Sam told him. "Jareem says he'll promise safety and forgiveness from his father if he in turn promises to renounce his forbidden sexuality and marry into a respectable family."

"So nothing's changed." John sighed. "Does the brother really think he can persuade Jareem?"

"They were very close growing up until Feisal joined the army. Jareem says Feisal became very moody and bitter during his service, especially against the US. He thinks that America is trying to strip Afghanistan of its culture and independence, trying to force the government to adopt American values. He wants the US troops to leave and the embassy to shut down. When he came home on leave, he was very critical of Jareem and his friends and their more liberal attitudes."

"Is Jareem surprised that his bro is coming to talk to him?"

"Yes, and he's not looking forward to it. He thinks the meeting will end badly, because he has no intention of going back with him. Which is what his father wants, of course. He is going to tell Feisal that he is staying here with me and that he will not agree to any kind of marriage just to please his father. That, of course, is going to piss Feisal off big time. One good thing I can tell you is that there hasn't been any more trouble from the men Mr. Durani hired to take Jareem back by force."

"But if Jareem refuses to go back with his brother, isn't that asking for trouble? Maybe the brother is in touch with the thugs over here."

"Yes, we've thought of that, but Agent Henderson and other FBI agents will be at the meeting, so there's no chance of Mr. Durani's men getting near him."

John wasn't so sure about that. In fact, he had a bad feeling about this 'meeting'.

"You've gone quiet," Sam remarked. "What is it?"

"I'm not sure. Where's the meeting to take place?"

"There's a restaurant in a park about two blocks from here, corner of Johnson and Clark. Henderson and three other agents will take us there. They don't expect Feisal to come alone, so safety in numbers, I guess."

"That's good. Okay, let me know how it went."

"Will do. How are things with you and Mark?"

"Good. He's happy 'cause he managed to wrap up a murder case and get a confession from one of the suspects. Still some legal stuff to follow up on, but it looks like they'll go to jail for a long time."

"That's good. Okay, I have to go. The agents are here to give us a briefing about the meeting with Feisal. I'll call you later and let you know how it went."

"Later, Sam… Oh, and tell Wallace I said hi."

Sam chuckled. "He's been reassigned. Jareem had a word with Henderson, telling him Wallace was rude…sneering at our relationship. Typical homophobe. Anyway, Henderson was okay with getting rid of him. I don't think they got along well. Henderson said Wallace had some crazy ideas of how the FBI should be run…weeding out those he considered unpatriotic or too liberal, which to him were apparently one and the same."

John snorted. "Why doesn't any of that surprise me? Okay, I'll let you go. We'll talk later so you can tell me all about the meeting. And, Sam, be careful."

"We will. Later, John, and thanks."

After they'd disconnected, John began to worry again. His gut was telling him something didn't feel right, and as usual, when he got these feelings, he couldn't ignore them. He knew better than to argue with his gut. It had to be warning him about the meeting between Jareem and his brother, Feisal. But why would there be any problems when there would be skilled, professional agents on hand to ensure everything went according to plan?

He sighed and stood away from his desk. At least Millie wasn't there to question him about where he was going. For some reason, he knew he had to be at the park. Not to get involved, of course. Just so he could keep an eye on the proceedings and be there to help Sam and Jareem if anything went wrong. But why should anything go wrong—was he over-reacting? Probably, but he would never forgive himself if either man got hurt…or worse. Sam and Jareem had come a long way, putting both their lives on the line to be together. They deserved to have a life free from the constant threat of a parent who believed that an honor killing was a just punishment for a love he could not understand or condone.

No way!

Grabbing his keys, helmet and leather jacket, he made for the door.

* * * *

Traffic was heavy on the freeway, but he made it to the park in good time. He drove around the perimeter, checking for exits and entrances, and found only two—the main park entrance on Johnson Avenue, the one that led to the restaurant's parking lot, and a smaller entrance on Clark. It wasn't a big park, and at this time of day it was mostly deserted. The restaurant was closed and there weren't any kiddie swings, which John decided was a good thing. There was an area of tall trees at the far end of the park, fronted by a large pond where some ducks were lazily swimming. The restaurant was situated on a small rise near the trees. A nice setting, but one that exposed the glass-lined dining room to anyone in the wooded area.

Not good.

He dismounted and rolled his bike into the cover of the trees. From there, he had a good view of the street, as well as the meeting place. About a half-hour later, a long black Mercedes limo pulled onto the driveway that led through the park to the restaurant. Four men got out. One, tall, with a military bearing, and younger than the other men, John guessed to be Feisal. He was dressed immaculately in a dark suit that John was sure was Armani. As the men looked around, two more cars joined them. A couple of agents climbed out of the first car, followed by Sam and Jareem.

The other car stopped and two more men joined the group. John recognized Henderson as one of the agents. Jareem walked toward his brother and embraced him. They spoke together in Arabic, then Feisal stepped back from Jareem, pointed at Sam and shouted at him. Sam, who obviously understood what was being said, gripped Jareem's arm and pulled him away from his brother.

Henderson held out his hands in a placating move. "Okay, let's settle down. We can go inside and listen to what Mr. Durani has to say."

"I can say it right here." Feisal spat out the words in a fury. "Jareem, my brother, was kidnapped by this infidel, seduced by him into thinking that the infidel loves him. He is being kept here against his will, and you Americans are enabling this criminal in his plan to bring our father nothing but heartache."

"You father only wants to punish Jareem," Sam rasped. "He has no heart to ache. Revenge is all he knows. Jareem will not return to Kabul with you, or any of your cronies. He is safe here and this is where he will stay—with me."

"Jareem!" Feisal ignored Sam. "My brother, you must come home. Our father prays each day that you will return to the bosom of our family. Don't defile yourself with this infidel. He will throw you aside when he's done with you."

"Stop, Feisal, you don't understand a thing." Jareem laid his hand over Sam's. "I will not return home, and neither should you go back to that oppressive society where your own father would kill you if you fell in love with a person he deems unfitting. Stay here in America with us and—"

"Have you gone mad?" Feisal all but screamed.

John was so caught up in the drama playing out before him that he almost missed the crunch of leaves to his right. He jerked his head toward the sound, and for a moment couldn't believe what he was seeing. A man, his face obscured by the shadows thrown by the tall trees, held a rifle with a telescopic lens, and it was aimed directly at Sam. *What the—?*

Quickly, he slid his gun from his shoulder holster then, using all his hunting skills taught to him by his uncle when he was a boy on the Dakota reservation, moved silently behind the would-be killer and placed the barrel of his gun against the back of the man's head.

"Wouldn't do that if I were you, Agent Wallace," he said softly, close to the agent's ear.

Wallace froze then whirled around, a panicked expression marring his face. "*Fucker…*" He rammed the rifle butt into John's chest, but he was too close and the blow was weak, enough only to make John fall back a step. Wallace lunged, trying to get his hands around John's throat. John kneed him in the balls. Wallace howled and doubled over, giving John the chance to whack him on the side of his head with his gun. Wallace groaned and fell to his knees.

John yelled, "Agent Henderson, better get over here, pronto."

"Get up," John snapped at Wallace as Henderson arrived, gun drawn.

"What's going on?" He gaped at Wallace and John.

"Seems like he wanted to put a bullet in Sam," John told him.

"He's lying," Wallace snarled, trying to get up.

John pushed him back down. "There's the rifle. His prints will be all over it. Better tell your men to watch Feisal and his entourage for any—" A shot rang out, cutting John off. He grabbed Wallace by his jacket collar and yanked him to his feet as Henderson ran to check out what was going on.

John pushed Wallace forward, using his gun to prod the small of the agent's back as encouragement to keep moving. When they reached the scene, one of Feisal's men was lying of the ground, moaning. The others had their hands up while the agents disarmed them.

"I've called for backup," an agent told Henderson.

"You were going to force me at gunpoint into going back with you?" Jareem raged at his brother. "Using guns, threatening us. You're my *brother*. How could you do this?"

"Father said he would punish me if I came back without you." Feisal startled then flinched when he caught sight of Wallace being pushed forward by John.

His reaction made it all clear to John. "Like to tell us about the connection between the two of you?"

"How dare you—there is no connection," Feisal gritted out. "I have never seen this man before."

Wallace tried to wrench himself from the grip John still had on his jacket collar, but without success. "You're lying." It was obvious from his angry and betrayed expression that Wallace realized his career was over and a long prison sentence was clearly in his future. "You hired me to take Sam Andrews out. With him dead, you figured your brother would agree to return home."

Henderson stared at Wallace in disbelief. "What the fuck were you thinking?" He motioned to one of the agents, who quickly handcuffed Wallace. John was happy to step away from the agent. His nervous sweat had made him smell rank.

"You paid this man to kill Sam?" Jareem looked as if he might strike his brother, who backed away from him. "Go back to Father and tell him you have failed, and tell him that I will never return home. I no longer have a brother, or a father. My home is here with Sam. Tell him that, Feisal, but never speak another word to me."

John almost felt sorry for Feisal. He stood, his shoulders hunched in defeat, staring at Jareem, who had turned away and was walking back to the federal agents' car, his arm around Sam's waist. An armored vehicle arrived on the scene in answer to the call for backup. Feisal's men were rounded up and pushed inside, the wounded man and Feisal along with them. He protested loudly, refusing, he said, to be treated like an animal. He was the son of a very rich and important man and all involved in this insult would pay dearly. His threats went unheard when the door of the armored vehicle slammed shut.

Sam and Jareem stood by the car, Jareem's face buried in Sam's chest as if he had tried to block the sounds of his brother's impotent rage. Sam stroked Jareem's hair and whispered in his ear, and John hoped Sam's words of comfort would be enough to help Jareem get over his family's lack of love for him.

After heaving a long sigh, Henderson gave John a narrowed-eye glare. "So how come you were here to save the day?"

John chuckled. "Sam told me about the meeting, and I had a feeling things weren't exactly kosher. I have to say, I was shocked to see Wallace with a sniper rifle in his hands. I don't like the guy, but I didn't peg him for a traitor slash assassin."

Henderson nodded. "I don't care for him either, but like you, I didn't see this coming."

"So this meeting was simply a ploy on Feisal's part to set up the killing of Sam Andrews," John said. "There was no sign that he had somehow gotten to Wallace to arrange the kill?"

"None whatsoever. Of course, now that Wallace is arrested, we'll have access to his computer and phone. They will no doubt answer the questions we all have."

John nodded. "What will happen now?"

"Quickest way to deal with it is to send Feisal back to his loving father, deport the guys associated with him and have the father paid a visit by officials from the embassy in Kabul. He thinks he has the backing of the chief of police, but that guy will part company with him if he feels his position is threatened. Bad as things are over there, we still have some say in who stays in power."

"Good to know. What'll happen to Wallace?"

"He can say goodbye to creature comforts for a long time."

"And Sam and Jareem?"

"I really wanted them to take on new identities—safer that way—but they won't go for it. Sam wants to continue with his lecture tours and archeological digs and Jareem wants to be by his side." He gave John a small smile. "And I can't blame him for that."

John returned Henderson's smile. "Did you just out yourself to me?"

"Guess I did," Henderson said wryly. "But don't worry, I'm not about to try and get between those two. Not that I would have much of a chance. They're made for each other, in my opinion. What they've been through to be together is one for the books."

"Can't argue with that. D'you need me to make a statement or anything?"

"I'll be in touch. We have to get Wallace arraigned and listen to him spill his guts, plus get Feisal and his gang put away until we can talk to a judge. So, unless you want to hang around the office for the rest of the day, I'd head home if I were you."

"Sounds like a good idea. I'll just say hi and goodbye to Sam and Jareem if that's okay."

"Sure thing. I'll call you when we need you."

John shook hands with Henderson, then walked over to where Sam and Jareem stood waiting to be taken back to the safe house. Sam gave him a big smile and a hug, while Jareem gazed at him through tear-laden eyes.

"We have to thank you again, John, for looking out for us," Sam said, patting him on the back. "We never reckoned on Feisal going to such lengths to please his father."

Jareem stroked John's arm. "I thank you also. You saved Samuel's life. Thanks are not enough, but it's all I have right now."

"Add a hug and we're even," John said chuckling. Jareem stepped into John's embrace and kissed him on both cheeks.

"Allah loves you," he whispered. "As do both Sam and I."

"Thank you," John said, touched by the young Arab's affectionate words. "Once all this is wrapped up, we can get together properly."

"We'll look forward to it." Sam started to smile, but grimaced instead as two agents marched Wallace over to their car and shove him, not at all gently, inside. "What a fool," he murmured.

"Well, he's gonna have lots of time to feel mad at himself," John remarked. "As someone once said, there's no antidote for stupid."

Epilogue

One month later

It had taken some time and reams of paperwork, but the FBI had finally deemed it safe for Sam and Jareem to leave the department's protection and go back to Sam's apartment in Silverlake. The religious sect had been rounded up and were in jail awaiting deportation. An official from the American embassy in Kabul had, with the chief of police, visited Jareem's father and warned him that any future threats of honor killing would be handled by the police department and reported to the local media. Not wanting to have the humiliation of having his son's sexual proclivities revealed in the newspaper, Mr. Durani, had, with a degree of surliness, agreed to back off.

Sid Renner had been given a life sentence, along with Chaz Martin. Ronnie Charleston, after turning state's evidence and throwing both Renner and Martin under the bus for the murder of Alex Vasquez, had received only a three-year sentence. John figured the three years would be sheer hell for the young redhead. When word got out that he'd squealed to get the lighter sentence, the other inmates would take great delight in having him wish he'd never opened his mouth.

"Hey, number two son," Jack yelled from where he was standing flipping his special steaks on the barbecue. "Take over here while I say hello to your charming secretary." He grinned at John. "Don't act so surprised. I do know how to treat a lady, you know."

"I don't doubt it," John replied cheekily. "Just don't treat her so well that she'll want to quit her job and leave me lost and alone."

Jack laughed and handed John the spatula. "Just don't let 'em burn, or you'll never get my secret recipe."

He wandered over to where Millie was in conversation with Audrey Melville, Sam and Jareem. With everything that had been going on, John had forgotten to mention to Mark that he thought Jack had the hots for Millie. Did older people get the hots for one another, or was Jack merely showing a gentlemanly interest? Millie certainly looked happy to see Jack. *The dear man*, she'd called him.

He leaned into Mark's strong body when his husband slipped an arm around his waist. "You okay here?"

"Of course. We prairie folk have been cooking over hot coals for centuries, you know."

Mark snorted. "When were you ever on the prairie doin' any kind of cooking? I'm amazed Dad let you near his famous steaks, knowing your reputation for not being able to even scramble an egg."

"Huh, I shall ignore that nasty comment and have you pay attention to your father and my secretary in deep and intimate conversation."

"Hardly deep and intimate with Audrey, Sam and Jareem listening in," Mark pointed out.

"Right. You'd think they'd have the sense to step away and let Jack work his magic."

"What on earth are you talking about?"

"Jack and Millie…they admire each other. Jack said she was intelligent and attractive, and Millie calls him 'the dear man'."

Mark stared at him and shook his head. "And from that you deduce they are interested in each other?"

"Yeah, why not?"

"Well, for one thing, looking at my dad paying very close attention to what Audrey is saying and laughing every two seconds, I'd say he was more interested in Audrey. Another lady who is intelligent and attractive."

"Really?"

"John, you have known my dad for ten years. You know he charms just about everyone he meets, especially the ladies. But I can assure you, because he's told me, Mom is irreplaceable in his eyes."

"Yeah, that's sweet." John kissed Mark's cheek. "Like you."

"I'm sweet?"

"No, I mean yes—but what I really meant was you're irreplaceable in my eyes."

Before Mark could react, Sam and Jareem walked over, looking happy and relaxed. "Hope we're not interrupting anything," Sam said, grinning. "You two look ready to jump each other's bones."

"Yeah, I know." John chuckled. "Even after all this time, he just can't get enough of me."

"John," Mark growled, his face flushed.

"I think it is wonderful," Jareem said. "I hope Samuel and I will be happy like you in the many years ahead."

"We will, sweetheart," Sam murmured close to Jareem's ear. "I promise you."

"Have you and Penny worked things out between you?" John asked Sam.

"She's coming around, I think," Sam replied. "The three of us went for lunch yesterday. We'd only talked on the phone prior to that. I wanted her to make the first move about getting together, and she finally did. It was awkward at first, as you can imagine. Penny having lunch with her brother and his boyfriend, something I'm sure she had never envisioned. We made a date for when Jareem and I come back from my lecture tour. We'll be gone for three weeks."

"She is a very sad lady," Jareem said. "And resentful that she has to share Sam with me. I have told Sam he can meet her on his own to make her happy."

"Which I won't do." Sam pulled Jareem closer to him. "Penny has to understand we're a couple now. I'm sure, in time, she'll get used to that, something that our father never will. He's refused every one of my calls, which I have to admit have only been two…but still."

"You're not working with him anymore?" Mark asked.

"No, I quit. No way could I have put up with the atmosphere he'd have created with us both in the same office." He sighed. "But enough of that, we're here to have a good time…and those steaks smell delicious."

"Mark…" John gave him a shove. "Go get Dad over here. These are done and I don't want them to burn. He'd never forgive me."

Mark chuckled, but went over to where Jack was still in Millie and Audrey's company. A few moments later, they had gathered around the barbecue. "Help yourselves to salad." Jack waved the spatula at a large bowl standing in a bucket of ice. John handed out plates, and before long everyone was seated at Jack's big patio table, enjoying steaks and one another's company.

* * * *

On their way home, John said, "You know this is nice, not like the last time we were over at Dad's and you made me take my bike so we couldn't drive together."

"I didn't *make* you take your bike. I thought I was going to be late, so I said I'd meet you at Dad's."

"Yes, but I couldn't...you know, *pleasure* you while you drove." John slipped his hand over Mark's thigh and inched his way onto Mark's crotch.

"John, that's a dangerous thing to do while I'm driving. I could get distracted and—"

"Oh, you'll get distracted all right...in the best possible way." He found Mark's zipper and yanked it down, then pushed his hand inside so he could squeeze and massage Mark's balls.

"John..."

"Feels good, doesn't it?" He leaned over and kissed Mark's neck. "Yes?" He could feel Mark's cock taking a great deal of interest in what he was doing.

"Yes," Mark groaned.

"Gonna feel even better any second now." He released Mark's erection from his briefs then lowered his head so he could take the hard, pulsing flesh into his mouth.

"John, you're gonna kill me..." He threaded his fingers through John's hair. "But don't stop."

"Mmm..." John hummed as he teased the glistening slit with the tip of his tongue. He peeked up at the expression of ecstasy on Mark's gorgeous face. "Never gonna stop, *mahasani*. Gonna hold you close and never stop loving you."

Want to see more from this author? Here's a taster for you to enjoy!

Hot in the Saddle: Vetting the Cowboy

J.P. Bowie

Excerpt

Parker Jones stared at the empty stalls in the stable with a look of disgust. "Randy? You in here somewhere? Randy?"

No reply came from anywhere in the large horse barn. Eight stalls stood empty, which was just as well—they were in dire need of mucking out. Horse manure and dirty straw had been trampled into the ground. Fortunately, the horses were either out in the pasture or being ridden by at least two new customers to Parker's dude ranch, the Seven Plus Ranch.

"What's up, boss?" It wasn't Randy answering, but Bob, one of Parker's older hands.

"You seen Randy?"

"No, I haven't. I thought maybe he'd called you, sayin' he was sick or somethin'."

"No, he didn't, but I've been on the phone for the last coupla hours with the bank, so he maybe couldn't get through." *At least I hope that's what it was. If he starts sneakin' out on me again…* Last week Randy had been a no-show two days running, and when Parker had asked him for an explanation, he'd become belligerent.

He hadn't gone so far as telling Parker it was none of his business, but Parker had guessed from his expression that it was foremost in his mind.

"Trouble?" Bob gave him a worried look. "About the bank, I mean."

"No, just some new stuff they want to throw my way. A lot of perks if I invest some more money. The usual."

Bob chuckled. "I wouldn't know about that."

"Right...well, those stalls need mucking out pronto, before the stink becomes obnoxious. I know the customers expect a ranch to smell like horses, but not that much horseshit."

"I'll get one of the guys to help me."

"No, I need them tending to the horses out on the pasture. I'll give you a hand."

"You, boss?"

"Yes, me boss. The day I think I'm too good to muck out a stall is the day I'll call it quits. Now, let's get on with it before they bring any of the horses back. There's a good two or three hours of work here."

Parker had a feeling Randy was on his way out but didn't have the guts to say so. He'd been surly the last couple of days and had shown up late without much of an apology. In Parker's opinion, Randy had a bunch of anger issues and needed counseling. Parker considered himself a laidback kind of guy and didn't ask his men to do anything he wouldn't do himself, but he did require a certain amount of diligence, and he absolutely hated tardiness and no-shows.

Running a dude ranch hadn't been Parker's burning ambition. It had been Royce's idea in the beginning, but his enthusiasm had won Parker over and, since they'd opened it six years ago, they'd had their share of success. Guys—and some women too—came from all over for a taste of the old west, chaperoned by Parker's experienced cowboys, who made sure nobody did anything rash or hurt any of the horses. In the early days, there had been one or two incidents that had made Parker glad Royce had insisted on really good insurance. But Royce was an attorney and clever as all get-out, so Parker was in good hands there.

Really good hands, it so happened, and had been for the past ten years. Parker smiled to himself, recalling how much his life had changed since he and Royce had hooked up, moved in together and finally bought their own home and ranch. They'd had their ups and downs, just like most everyone, but they had figured out early on that the way to harmony was to talk out their differences of opinion before they became major problems.

His cell phone chiming in his jeans' back pocket had him grinning. *Bound to be Royce.* It was that time of the day.

"Hi, handsome."

"You sound chipper," Royce teased.

"Must be the sound of your voice. Right now I'm muckin' out the stalls 'cause some lazy fucker didn't show…again."

"Would that lazy fucker be Randy?"

"Right first time." Parker sighed. "Gotta feelin' I'm gonna have to show him the gate."

"Would that be so bad?"

"Not really, but I'll have to find a replacement. This old back of mine isn't taking kindly to physical labor, I don't mind telling you."

"Thirty-eight is not old, Parker. If you didn't go around falling off horses all the time, your back would be just dandy."

"All the time? I can count on one hand the amount of times I've been thrown, and one of them was your fault."

Royce laughed. "Oh, not that old story again."

"Well, it's true. You strutting around with your cute little ass in those tight, tight jeans and pretending to be so high and mighty put me in a mood, so I wasn't paying attention to what I should've been doing!"

"Excuses, excuses. Anyway, how bad is your back? Can't you get one of the guys to take over?"

"Bob's helping, but I want to keep the other guys with the horses and there's two customers getting riding lessons. We're almost done anyway. I'll have Bob hose down then we can get the clean straw laid."

"Well, take it easy after. Remember, you still have your husbandly duties to take care of when I get home."

Parker groaned. "Again?"

"Yes, again...and again."

"You are insatiable," Parker said through his laughter.

"And you are one lucky man. Okay, I'll let you get back to your mucking."

"Ciao, baby."

"Ciao, daddy."

Parker was still grinning when he shut his phone off. "That Royce?" Bob asked.

"Yessir. Checkin' up on me, making sure I'm workin' hard."

"No doubt of that." Bob leaned on his rake for a moment. "For a man that owns and runs this place, never saw anyone work harder than you."

"Lookin' for a raise, Bob?"

"No, sir...but if you're offerin'..."

"Not the right time of year, Bob," Parker said grinning at the older man. "'N'other coupla months." He turned at the clatter of hooves behind him. "Hold up, Seth. We're not done with all the stalls yet."

"Bonney's limping some," tall, blond Seth Archer told him. "Thought I'd bring her in for a looksee."

"Oh, okay, let me do that."

"Left foreleg, I think—seems to be favoring it a bit."

Parker knelt in front of the mare and ran his hands up and down her leg. Bonney, one of their calmer horses, and popular with newbies, stood patiently while Parker did a quick examination. She whinnied softly when Parker lifted her hoof off the ground to take a look.

"Here's the problem. Looks like an abscess. Better call Doc. Walker, have him give us an opinion. Don't want to mess with something like this...might be nasty." Parker frowned. "We better check all the horses, limping or not, just in case."

"Okay, boss." Seth paused then asked, "Why are you cleaning out the stalls? Where's Randy?"

Parker straightened and gave the handsome cowboy a rueful look. "No-show, so Bob and me took over. Place was a pigsty. Seems like he's been neglecting his duties lately."

"Yeah, he's a bit slapdash at times."

Parker grunted. "Well, my fault too. I usually come around at the end of the day to make sure they're all bedded down nice, but the last couple of nights we've been busy entertaining some maybe investors. Bad excuse, and one I won't be using again."

"Well, if you're busy any time, just give me a call and I'll stop by and check up on them. I live nearby."

"Thanks, Seth, appreciate it. Call Doc. Walker for me while I clean up here, and have him come over soon as he can."

"Will do." Seth pulled his cell from his back pocket and punched in the doctor's number. All the hands had the vet's contact programmed into their phones for emergencies. "Hey, Doc, Seth over at Seven Plus Ranch. Parker asked if you come check up on one of the horses. Bonney…she's limping and Parker think it might be an abscess. Oh, right…that's good, see you later."

About the Author

J.P. Bowie was born in Scotland and toured British theatres in numerous musical shows including Stephen Sondheim's Company.

He emigrated to the States and worked in Las Vegas, Nevada for the magicians Siegfried and Roy as their Head of Wardrobe at the Mirage Hotel. He is currently living with his husband in sunny San Diego, California.

J.P. Bowie loves to hear from readers. You can find his contact information, website details and author profile page at https://www.pride-publishing.com

www.ingramcontent.com/pod-product-compliance
Lightning Source LLC
LaVergne TN
LVHW090938080826
845145LV00003B/794

* 9 7 8 1 8 3 9 4 3 9 8 6 5 *